RAW
PRAYER
REQUESTS

Raw Prayer Requests

THE REQUESTS THAT REMAIN UNSPOKEN

Samantha Gillion

Debra Palmer

To Mr. Gillion and the Jayz. You all are the reason for my drive. There is no Samantha Gillion without you.

To Mr. Gillion, my Man of God. You were beautifully created in God's image. You are my private warrior, ready to jump when needed. Many question my motive for remaining on this path with you. I answer because this path was designed for me by God and He continues to walk with me. I thank God that as we grow old together, our hearts become one beat with one sound. I love you and our children always.

Meet the author Samantha Gillion

"Have I not commanded you? Be strong and of good courage; do not be afraid, nor be dismayed, for the Lord your God is with you wherever you go." Joshua 1:9

Hello! My name is Samantha Gillion. I am the author and founder of Raw Prayer Requests, a wife and mother of six vibrant children. Raw Prayer Requests, R.P.R., is a movement. This movement was established because of my own R.P.R. I walked daily with feelings of depression and anxiety. I felt as if keeping quiet would protect me from the judgment and ridicule of others. It was during my morning devotions God began to share with me. He showed me I was not alone. Others identify and suffer in the same silence. **Ecclesiastes 4:9-10 tells us that, "Two are better than one because they have a good return for their labor: If either of them falls, one can help the other up. But pity anyone who falls and has no one to help them up."**

My goal is to encourage those who struggle while providing non-judgmental support for those wishing to reveal their truth and regain their freedom. I've learned that a **Raw Prayer Request** continues to keep one silent, unlike a "pray request" that only reveals the surface issue.

Like many, I would make my way down the long aisle to the altar for prayer only to state a surface prayer request. The one I felt would be approved by others. I was afraid that if I told the raw truth in my prayer request that I would be judged or spoken about negatively. I remained silent for years. I never realized that I was placing myself in bondage and that my prayers could never honestly be answered if I remained silent. **Death and life are in the power of the tongue: and they that love it shall eat the fruit thereof, Proverbs 18:21.** I needed to speak my truth to regain control over my life. If one does not truly understand why one is seeking prayer, one cannot correctly go to God on one's behalf. Why? Because they are only praying for the surface, and most of our true requests are deeply rooted and need one to go deep to uproot them. Why do you think people often suffer from depression, anxiety, sleepless nights, or insecurities? One suffers because their Raw Prayer Requests are hidden within their body's strongest muscle, their heart.

My story is still being written. Each day I wake ready to begin my spiritual war. I encourage all who struggle daily with a rawness to join the fight to conquer and take those demons out. I pray my story gives you permission to fight and never give up on God-ordained visions. I want to leave you with one of my favorite quotes and scriptures. I have learned that speaking life into a challenging situation gives one encouragement to continue the push. *"You have to help me; you have to stand"-Belle... Beauty* and *the Beast.* If one is not willing to stand in the fight, how can one overcome it? *Have I not commanded you? Be strong and courageous. Do not be afraid; do not be discouraged; for the LORD, your God will be with you wherever you go. Joshua 1:9*

I am overly excited for you to meet and read the story of Proof and Scar. Proof and Scar are fictitious characters birthed from my own personal Raw Prayer Requests within my marriage's hidden parts. Proof is one that hides behind her children and career in hopes of her truth remaining concealed. Many see Proof and assume she is the model mentor of goals and achievements. She has the home, a beautiful family, and a promising career. However, she struggles daily with the reality of being a single, married individual. Daily she wakes to the reality of her husband's absence. She battles with thoughts of insecurities and unanswered questions. Proof spends most of her free time in her untouchable war zone, her prayer closet, fighting for her happily ever after. She knows that God will honor his word and save her marriage; therefore, she must remain in this fight. Proof will then be ***proof*** that God can and will change any situation. Scar, however, is fed up with Proof and her prayers. Scar is in-love with Proof and his children, but the back-and-forth with Proof has grown old. At the beginning of their marriage, Scar was ready to become the model husband and willing to do whatever needed to please Proof. However, over time, Proof's numerous choices to abandon their marriage left ***scars*** that Scar feels are not worth repairing. Each time Proof chose to neglect their marriage and leave, Scar is forced to deal with severe rejection issues. He would instead choose to remain alone away from the betrayal of Proof and her God-fearing prayer life. I pray that both Proof and Scar's rawness will persuade you to become free of your rawness and rejection feelings.

The Absence of a Father

The Absence of a Father

Your absence is like an asthma attack,
I'm suffocating on my pride,
I want to call you,
Instead, I'll just hold in my cry,
The memories we made,
I feel so loved,
I want to make more,
But we dodge and we shove,
Your absence never bothered me,
Until my senior year,
I have matured into a young man,
And you're not here,
My mother has been my father,
It's so hard to say,
She has raised a strong spirit,
While you found your escape,
Now I'm leaving for college,
I want to reconnect,
Even though you were not in my life,
Don't let my brothers be next.

Jay•en Gillion 2020

1

Solomon 3:2

Chapter 1

*"I will get up now and go about the city, through its streets and squares;
I will search for the one my heart loves. So I looked for him but did not find
him". Song of Solomon 3:2*

Finally, Proof was able to fall asleep. She had been up all night praying and asking God,"Why?" Why her? Why her children? Why now? She and her husband had been doing so well. At last, she felt they were becoming a unit. They began communicating again and raising their children as a team. She never imagined that she would be in this boat alone yet still. This was the second year she had been away from her husband or felt his presence beside her.

Long nights had become a regular experience for Proof. Nights were safe; they allowedProof to be alone and uninterrupted with her rawness. The quiet safety of the night permitted Proof time to be alone with her memories. She often fell asleep to visions of the reconciliation of her marriage. She prayed nightly for her husband's return and the restoration of her family. The feeling of emptiness began to develop into a numbing pain that was far from healing.

A sudden sound from the dryer door opening woke her. It was already time to begin her day. Her son was preparing for church. She opened her eyes barely and whispered, "Get it together Proof; there's no need for him to know or see." Good morning Momma, he said. Proof was determined to keep her nightly cries confined to the four walls of her bedroom. There was no need for them to escape throughout the peacefulness of her home.

"Good morning, son. How did you sleep last night?" asked Proof. She always asked how her children slept. Good sleep was priceless, and she wanted them to know she cared about their rest.

"I slept okay, but my neck hurts from the way I was lying," he replied. Proof purposely left the room without light because she did not want her son to see the washed-out look on her face from the night cries.

It was Sunday, her favorite day of the week. Sundays were family days, and she loved going to church with her family and not worrying about a schedule. She wiped her face as her son walked away and headed to the bathroom to prep for the day. The night cries were over; for now, she knew it was time to put her face on and begin this beautiful day with her partial family.

Proof was the type of woman who kept those raw places hidden from view. As far as the world knew, she was a beautiful and quiet spirit. She purposely went out of her way to make sure her appearance never revealed her truth. Proof worked out religiously and only wore the most exquisite shoes and clothing. Her image meant everything to her, and she never wanted anyone to notice her pain from her appearance. Everyone knew that something was not quite right because her husband was never around, and she always made excuses about where he was and what he was doing. However, as long as they kept their thoughts private, she was okay with individuals' judgmental looks. She would never confirm or deny anything. She made a vow to herself when her husband dismissed himself from their marriage that she would not be anyone's Sunday roundtable discussion. Therefore her raw parts remained locked. She did not even dare to ask for prayers for her husband because she knew the unspoken opinions that would erupt from her prayer requests.

Proof and her husband Scar were a family of Ten. Together Scar and Proof shared six children, and Scar had two children that were created out of his infidelities. Proof took him back after each child because she was committed to him through their marriage vows that she was unwilling to break. Scar and Proof shared eighteen years of marriage, and after all, God always held her down; she did not want for anything. She had the house, cars, and her children were very well taken care of. Seeing Proof out with her family, one would think she was off the runway with a husband who held down a multi-million dollar office job, as she preferred.

Proof worked hard in her studies. She and Scar struggled financially at the beginning of their marriage. Proof was determined to complete whatever studies needed to live a fabulous lifestyle. With her master's in education, she had become one of the most well-known principals in her city. She had a waiting list for entries into her school, and residents in the surrounding area quickly learned that kindergarten entry was the only guaranteed way to get a coveted spot for their child. Proof also convinced Scar to complete his master's in business. He was successful in owning his own event rental company. Scar's rental company was also well known. The Lord blessed his business to service areas outside the surrounding areas. Scar often traveled to other cities and states to set up various events.

As Proof was in the shower with her thoughts, she could hear her younger daughter's footsteps. "Momma," she screamed. Her scream rattled Proof as she had escaped somewhere else. Proof could only laugh to herself. She always said, *if I nee* a chil*, get nake*.*

"Yes, girl," she answered, annoyed. She already knew it could not be much. Her children, at times, acted helpless without her assistance.

"What am I wearing today?" she asked as she stood there with her hands on her hips. Proof had to think for a moment. She was never one to be as prepared as she should be, which caused her to scramble. Because of her night, she had not even given any thought to clothes.

"Put on your black dress with pink polka-dots," she answered. Proof suggested the first thing that came to her mind. She was eager to finish her last thoughts alone before she had to become a super mom and pretend she was content with her reality.

"Momma, I wore that last week," she answered sternly because now she was annoyed. Proof knew that just throwing up an answer would not get rid of this child. She had to become quicker on her feet.

"Oh! I forgot, put on your pink sundress with the white flowers", Proof responded. She ran out to retrieve the dress. Proof quickly got out of the shower, keeping in mind that church would begin soon, and she did not want to be late. She could hear that all six babies were up getting ready for the day. Her oldest two were excellent leaders. Her son woke everyone and was in the process of getting them all something to eat before they left, while her daughter was combing hair.

She sat on her bed, thanking God for her children and how much of a gift they all were. She quickly sprung up and went to her beautiful walk-in closet to grab her Giorgio Armani jumpsuit. After having a night as she had just encountered, she wanted to be cute but yet comfortable. She stood in her closet for a moment, and her mind began to wander once more. For some strange reason, she could not shake the thoughts of her husband today. They were more robust than ever before, and it was overwhelming. She quickly shook them off, gathered herself, grabbed her things, and began to dress for this beautiful Sunday. "Momma," she heard the entire crew scream. The scream irritated Proof. She could only imagine who had suffered a hit or had something taken away. She quickly took a deep breath and whispered, "Proof it is not their fault if Scar is not here."

"Yes," she responded,

"We are ready."

Proof was relieved to hear that no one was bleeding or tormenting someone else. She walked over to her floor-length mirror in the bedroom to get one last look. The woman staring back at her had no resemblance to the women that lived within her. As she stood there, she began to whisper affirmations over herself, "Proof you will have the victory," "You will be courageous," "You are an excellent mother," "You will overcome this." As she grabbed her *Louis Vuitton* bag, she thought, *Thank Go♦ my chil♦ren are traine♦ well enough to navigate without me hovering over them.*

The church was packed today, and there was barely any parking for miles. Proof attended one of the biggest churches within her city. She enjoyed this church because it was multicultural and gave her children options to serve and worship God naturally. Proof was real ample to allow her children to feel their own experience with God; therefore, she allowed them to participate in the church's various life groups. She was over a life group of ninth-graders, but she felt it necessary to be fed before feeding anyone else. She decided long ago she was a lover of Christ and His promises and was willing to allow Him into her heart no matter what needed to be shredded. She quickly spotted a parking space, pulled in, and prepared for the long hike ahead.

Upon entry to the church, she was greeted by the welcome committee, who always gave the warmest hugs and smiles needed every Sunday after her long, grueling weeks. She took each of her children and kissed them all before they each hurried to their designated areas.

As she entered the sanctuary, the presence of God immediately greeted her. It was refreshing. She felt as if God was standing there, waiting to walk her to her seat. After only a few moments, she realized why the parking was so painful. She had forgotten that today her church was beginning a marriage series titled, *What Ma♦e You Say, "I ♦o"?* And the guest speaker was none other than the marriage guru himself, Gary Thomas. Of course, this made Proof excited. She had read almost every book he had written about marriage and relationships. She thought to herself, "After a night like last night, only my God knew what I needed." The series was going to be taught over a series of weeks, and Gary Thomas was the kick-off speaker. She only wished her husband would come to at least one, but she knew he would not. Scar was not the type to attend church even when he was home. He only came to church when he thought Proof would leave him, and for him, that too had grown old. As she reviewed her church program, she began to skim the questions presented over the coming weeks. As Proof sat there in anticipation, she couldn't help but think, *this is right on time.*

2

Philippians 2:3-4

Chapter 2

Do you attempt to put your spouse's needs ahead of your own?
"Do nothing from selfish ambition or conceit, but in humility,
count others more significant than yourselves. Let each of you look
not only to his interests but also to the interests of others." Philippi-
ans 2:3-4

The morning air smelled so delightful. Proof was in the middle of training for the upcoming half marathon. Some thought she was crazy, but the long runs cleared her mind and allowed her to escape with God. Plus, having a hobby like running was great for her soul and image. Proof's past week was full of stress from standardized tests preparation, parent meetings, and still no communication with her husband. She needed this moment of escape. As she ended her stretches, she took off for her long-awaited time of escape. Proof loved to run in her neighborhood because it offered priceless scenery. As her feet hit the pavement one after the other, she could not help but reflect on the topic from the past Sunday, *"Do you attempt to put your spouse's nee♦s ahea♦ of your own?"* She could not resist going back to the beginning of her and Scar's relationship before they married.

October 1999

"How was your day today?" Scar asked. Proof had been at work all day. She worked at a major department store in the shoe department. Unfortunately, she was required to stand for long hours a time, rarely receiving a break because of how steady the store remained. Her favorite part of her workday was coming home to Scar, relaxing, and releasing the day's tension. Scar was so in tune with Proof, and he prided himself in meeting her every need.

"It was okay, I guess. I watched a kid perform a massive fit because her mom would not buy her a pair of $85 shoes", Proof responded. "Are you going to work tonight?" she asked.

Scar worked nights, which Proof loathed. Scar being gone forced her to sleep alone, which she dreaded. In his absence, she would often sleep on the couch because she hated rolling over to emptiness; therefore, the nights he was off were a welcoming delight. Both would stay up to watch movies or play games. However, most nights ended with Proof falling asleep in the warmth of Scar's arms.

"Naw, they closed the factory cause it's too cold to work," Scar responded. Proof hated his grammar. If she could write him a script for his responses, she would. She desired for Scar to be his best. She saw so much potential in him, and she yearned for him to reach it. She understood he became annoyed; however, she felt if she continued the push, he would change and adapt.

"Because it is too cold outside," she corrected.

"Whatever, you know what da hell I mean," Scar snapped back.

There was no use Proof thought. *He is always going to speak using improper grammar.* Since Scar was not going to work, he decided to shower and relax for the night. Proof decided to catch up on some television. The sound from Scar's shower was so relaxing. Proof felt herself slowly falling asleep. She could hear the people talking on the tv, but their voices quickly began to sound like white noise, and she was asleep before the first five minutes of her show.

Proof was awakened to the feel of Scar's warm lips on hers. It slightly startled her but only enough to make her eyes open. "Are you gonna go to sleep without a bath?" Scar asked. Proof knew all too well what that meant. She understood that she and Scar rarely had nights together. They both cherished these times. She knew she needed to get up because God only knew when Scar would have another night off.

"Of course not," she responded. She jumped to go fetch her bath. Her baths were one of her most favorite times of the day. She was alone with her thoughts and dreams without the shrewdness of others. She could go anywhere in her mind, and no one had control but her.

As she began to escape, she could feel Scar staring at her in the door. "What's up, Scar?" she said, slightly annoyed. If only she could fully understand Scar's heart toward her. She was everything to him plus. Scar would never share his hidden fears with Proof of not being able to please her fully. He would continue to orchestrate his quiet hustle with the thought of only pleasing his queen.

"I'm just looking. I can look, right?" Proof would not learn until later that Scar enjoyed becoming lost in her beauty. He turned and walked off. Proof continued her bath for another ten minutes uninterrupted, knowing that Scar's feelings were hurt, and she had only ten minutes before she could correct them. Once she returned to the room, Scar was sitting on the bed watching a football game. That was his favorite pastime. Proof attempted to disrupt him during but later learned to adjust to his seasonal escape.

"Lotion?" he asked.

"As always," she responded.

After long days Scar would always give Proof a much-needed massage. He knew how much it relaxed her, and he did not mind using the tools he had to comfort her. His hands were strong enough to remove all of her aches and pains.

Proof's run was coming to an end, and she regretted seeing her house in the distance because that meant her beautiful thoughts had to be put on hold. She ran into her driveway and hurried into the house to take a shower for dinner. As always, the sound of the water was relaxing and calming to her body. Proof enjoyed nothing more than a good run and shower to follow. It was the excuse needed to have more time with her memories.

"Momma, where are we going to eat?" Proof's thoughts were abruptly interrupted. She knew it was only a matter of time that one of her angels would arise with hunger pains.

"I honestly have not thought about it," she responded. "What sounds good?" "Momma, I don't know, you da momma!" her sassy daughter said. She was as sassy as they came. She had no problem standing her ground or stating her opinion.

"Well, let's go to my favorite," Proof hollered back.

She quickly finished her shower to get dressed and begin her night with her tiny dates.

Of course, spending time with her babies was a rare treat. During the week, her days were long and tiresome. She was not just the principal of her school. She was the nurse, janitor, counselor, police investigator, and rewarding days, the cook, and cafeteria monitor. There were so many demands from the district that she would often get home only with enough time to review homework, cook, and go to bed. If it were not for her older two children, Proof would probably be in an insane asylum. Her oldest two children were blessings in disguise. They were both selfless individuals who were willing to be a part of their mother's support team. Even though Proof attempted to conceal her reality, she was aware that her older children understood the truth behind her mask.

As the food arrived at their table, she and the kids held hands and prayed as they did over every meal. Proof had to stop her oldest three because they would always dig in before the youngest three could contribute to the prayer, which annoyed them every time.

"Have you talked to daddy today?" her oldest son asked. Proof decided a long time ago that what goes on between her and Scar had nothing to do with the relationship between him and his children. She made sure that he was aware of every recital, game, report card, doctor's appointment, and anything else that involved their children. "You need to talk to him, son," she said nervously.

Proof attempted as often as she could to remain unbothered with the mention of their father. She knew that her children could feel her demeanor change when he was mentioned. Each time she felt as if a knife was applied to her heart. She could feel lumps as they formed in her throat as she attempted to swallow them away.

"I do; I need him to know my schedule for the upcoming season," he stated. Her son was very active in sports, and Proof felt he needed support. But she knew she could not make Scar answer or come.

"Son, call him; he may be at work. If he doesn't answer, leave a message or text him," she stated. Proof attempted to be quick on her feet, trying hard not to let her facial expressions tell on her heart. She always gave a back-up alternative just in case Scar needed one. She never knew what Scar was up to, but she wanted her children to know that it was for a good reason if he did not respond.

Of course, Dinner was terrific, and Proof and the kids were all ready to retire home and begin planning for the week ahead. On the ride home, Proof could not help but slip back into the topic from the previous Sunday, *"Do you attempt to put your spouse's needs ahead of your own?"* besides, all of her children were occupied with phones or asleep. As she began to ponder, she could not help but wonder had she loved Scar selflessly. Had she always put his feelings before her own? Was he her priority?

September 2000

"Proof!" Scar hollered. What does he want now, Proof thought. He was always yelling. He knew she was in the middle of cooking.

"Yes," Proof hollered back. She could only imagine what his response was going to be. Proof was about five months pregnant, and Scar was wearing on her last nerve.

"Are there onions in this spaghetti?" Scar hated onions. *Of course, there are onions in the spaghetti,* she thought. *How else do you make spaghetti?* She knew that Scar hated them, but she had not learned how to add them without "adding them." Plus, she was tired of standing and ready to sit down. Proof had left the department store and was now working at a daycare. Being pregnant and watching over somebody else's children grew very old after about 5 p.m.

"Yes, Scar, there are onions in the spaghetti. How else do you make spaghetti?" Proof said, annoyed. *What ◆oes he want me to ◆o? Remove each onion one by one,* Proof thought.

Scar had a sarcasm like no one else. "Why does he not just see that I am trying? Why don't we ignore the fact that I am five months pregnant?" Proof said under her breath.

"You know how much I hate onions. I have asked you more than once not to put onions in my food. However, you keep doing it. What am I supposed to eat now, because I am not eating this shit!" he said as he walked out the door.

Proof was glad he left. He had been on her nerves all day. Nothing Proof did was correct. She was trying her hardest to be a submissive wife like the pastor said, but all Scar did was complain and criticize her. Proof knew that Scar would be gone for the night. She felt that he was just picking a fight to get out of the house. Lord only knew which lady would be chosen tonight to fulfill his needs.

————————————————————————————————————

"Momma, you passed the house," one of her children shouted. Proof had become so lost in her thoughts she forgot to turn. She often wondered if she chose her battle wisely in regards to the onions in Scar's food. After all she was preparing the food for him. The more she pondered, she recognized that she too had needs that Scar did not understand; however she still wanted him to at least attempt to.

"My fault," as she slowly turned around. Proof knew it was time to focus and get her babies home safe.

Proof and Scar had been blessed with a beautiful home; they had a five-bedroom, three and a half bath home. Their house came with a back and front yard to match the dreams they often talked about during late nights. However, the house felt empty because Proof was alone each night without her husband's warmth in her bed. She missed him more than words. She could not understand how a man could leave his family without notice.

Proof decided to venture to her prayer closet for answers. She knew where her thoughts would not be interrupted by small creatures because her children understood that she would not be bothered once that closet door closed. She settled her children and quickly made her way to her in-home prayer oasis.

Proof's prayer closet was small but comfortable. This was the only place in the world; she could show her vulnerability. Here she allowed her nakedness to be exposed. Only God understood her heart, and only God could help her with this mess. As soon as the door closed, God instructed her to create a prayer to hang on her wall about being submissive, allowing herself to die to herself daily. God told Proof to pray it daily over herself. God wanted Proof to understand that each day she represented His love for Scar through her actions.

Dear Heavenly Father,

*Thank you for the opportunity to be in your presence yet again. Thank you, Go♦, for my husban♦, Scar, my man of Go♦. Lor♦, you sai♦ in your wor♦ that as Scar's wife, I am to submit to him in everything I ♦o, for he is the hea♦ of my househol♦, accor♦ing to **Ephesians 5:22-33**. Thank You, Lor♦, for teaching me how to submit to Scar an♦ re♦irect my heart each time I fall short. Lor♦, thank You that I ♦ie to my flesh ♦aily, allowing you to fill me up. Thank You that Scar sees you, Go♦, in my responses an♦ actions towar♦ him.*

It is so. In the name of Jesus, I pray.

Amen

With tears streaming down her face and hope in her heart, she placed the prayer on her wall and fell asleep.

3

Proverbs 26:17

Chapter 3

How many others do you invite into your marital affairs?
"Interfering in someone else's argument is as foolish as yank-
ing a dog's ears".Proverbs 26:17

It had been a very hectic Monday morning at Proof's school. Already, Proof had been called to break up two fights, deal with a child
wearing the same clothes since the prior week, and three teachers were
out. She was overwhelmed. Proof rarely drank sodas; however, one was
calling her name loud and clear. After she got the last fight settled, she
made her way to the teachers' lounge. She rarely visited the lounge, not
because she didn't love her teachers or enjoy their conversation but because when Proof entered the room, her teachers got quiet, and everyone looked up as if to say, "is it me?" or "why is she here?" For that
reason, she allowed them to dine without her interference. As she entered the room, she could hear their day's conversation, but they all got
quiet as soon as they saw her and looked like deer in headlights. She
thought to herself, *why not?* She decided to spark a conversation.

"How is everyone's day going so far?" She asked. Proof wanted her
staff to feel she cared. Her desires were never to seem unreachable. She

wanted her team to respect her but also know that her door was always open.

One teacher looked puzzled while the other said, "This is the worst day of the year! Come on, summer." Proof had to agree, it was. She was just as ready for the summer and the much needed time with her family.

Proof needed a mental break, so she continued. "Do you have plans for the summer?" she asked. The change of scenery outside the office was welcoming. She rarely got the opportunity to escape the drama that the office held. There was always a new demanding occurrence that needed immediate attention.

"I do; I am getting married this summer," she smiled. Proof could feel the lump forming in her throat. New love is a fantastic thing. She remembered it all so well; she and Scar could not move without one another. At the beginning of their marriage, Proof loved just laying on Scar's chest, counting the beats in his heart. Scar's warm body was Proof's much-needed escape from her intense days. In the beginning, they didn't even sleep without holding hands.

"That is wonderful news. Marriage is hard work but worth it," Proof announced. Proof loved to mentor new couples. She felt that if she could save one marriage from some of the mistakes that she and Scar experienced, she would be doing something correctly. She thought about asking that teacher to visit her church, but as soon as the thought came to her, the fear of being questioned followed. *What if she wants to sit with me? What if she asks me where Scar is? What if she comes back to school an* shares it with everyone? She dismissed that thought as soon as it was formed. Proof could not stand the idea of being the topic of discussion. She attempted to remain as private as possible. She only opened to those God gave clearance to. She knew God sent them when they could reveal something only God would know.

"How long have you been married, Mrs. Moings?" she asked. "I have been married for eighteen years," she responded. Proof was proud that she and Scar had lasted for so long. They were high school sweethearts, and she never in a million years thought they would still be standing for this long.

"What is the secret?" she asked. People always wanted to know the secret. The truth was Proof honestly did not know. She and Scar had been through so many highs and lows that she had become overwhelmed with discovering the secret herself.

Proof gave her the same response that she gave all new couples. "Keep your marriage business to yourself," she said sternly. Proof had learned the hard way that it is no one's business what goes on in your marriage. The only soul that should know other than God is your spouse. Proof could hear her walkie-talkie going off. She thanked God for the escape. She quickly grabbed her soda and headed off.

The day had finally come to an end. Proof frequently stayed over to catch up on paperwork, but today she was leaving. She had had enough and needed a breath of fresh air. She quickly grabbed her things, said goodbye to her office staff, and left. Her drive home was one of the best parts of her day. She could escape to as many places as needed in her thoughts. She couldn't help but think about her brief conversation earlier. She wished that she and that teacher had been in another arena because Proof would have sat her down and gave it to her straight, but Proof rarely mixed business with pleasure. As far as her staff knew, she was over the moon in love with Scar, and they both shared a picture-perfect life. As the trees passed her windows, her thoughts began to overwhelm her. The previous topic at church was about sharing your marital business. Proof was now a lockbox on her marriage; however, she had to learn the hard way.

April 2002

Scar and Proof were living separately due to financial issues and were in the process of reuniting. Scar was living with relatives, and Proof was on her way to visit. She called Scar and told him she was coming, but something within her knew he would not be ready.

Proof arrived, and as predicted, "Scar fashion," he was not ready, his cousin confirmed. He was always up to something. He could never be prepared when she needed him to be. "Where is Scar?" Proof asked, irritated. Proof would never understand. If Scar knew she was coming, why did she have to wait on him?

"He is upstairs, working on something," his cousin responded. Suddenly Scar appeared with something in his hand. Proof could never honestly explain it, but when Scar entered the room, the irritating part of waiting always disappeared. Scar's presence would always turn Proof's scowl into the biggest smile. She could never genuinely be upset with him.

"Proof, where are you?" he hollered. Scar loved to mess with Proof. He found it funny and cute to get her upset.

"I am right here, boy!" she yelled. Proof was attempting to act still irritated. But Scar knew the effect he had on her. Her fake irritation just fueled him more.

"Here, read this and then wait," he instructed. This was not abnormal. Scar always wrote love letters or poems to Proof. That was how he expressed himself. They were a reminder to her that she was loved unconditionally. As she opened the letter, it read:

Dearest Proof

I am upstairs writing to you to tell you how I feel about you. You make me so ma· sometimes that I cannot stan· you, but for some reason, I still love you. When I am ma·, your smile breaks me ·own, an· I can't be ma· any longer...

"What are you reading?" his cousin shouted. Proof did not answer; she just walked away and continued reading.

I am so gla· that you are in my life. I forgive you for everything that you have ·one to me. I want you in my life so I can kiss you anytime I want to...

As Proof read, Scar ran in and kissed her on the forehead. He had the biggest smile on his face. Proof did not notice that he had been hiding behind the door the entire time. Scar liked to remain unpredictable. He loved aggressively. Others struggled to understand his love, but Proof understood it very well, and that was all that mattered.

"Did you read my letter?" He was so proud of his love for Proof. In the past, he struggled with loving others. She brought parts of him to the surface that he attempted to keep hidden. Scar was willing to be silly to keep her with constant smiles.

"Not all of it, but I am working on it," Proof answered. Scar ran off for her to finish.

Proof had to leave her thoughts because she was pulling up to pick up her youngest daughter. This little sweetheart was a huge surprise. Proof and Scar had the chance to complete a mission project over spring break, and upon return, Proof was carrying this little life. As she walked in, she could hear her tiny feet running toward her. She had been one of Proof's small raw prayer requests. She came at a time where others questioned why. Even though Proof chose not to share her marital affairs with others, Scar's absence was not a secret. Proof found it difficult to ask others to pray for something they shamed.

"Hey, sweet girl. How was your day, my love?" Proof quickly picked her daughter's little tiny body up. The hug around her neck from this gentle creature was exactly what Proof needed from this long day. Proof quickly spoke to everyone as she always did, grabbed her sweet angel, and left immediately to retrieve her other children. Picking up children used to be a Scar thing, and she missed it. These last two years brought on a new strain like none other. Picking up her children daily had become a task within itself.

Proof finally made it home from the long afternoon of playing the Uber driver. She wanted to buy take out, but she needed to save money; therefore, she had to cook. She did not cook as much because Scar was not at home. She took the easy way out, and the family either ate takeout or had a simple meal. She suddenly realized she forgot to take something out of the freezer; she thought to herself, *Hibachi it is.* She grabbed the phone, called in the order, and headed out to pick it up. She went alone to gather her thoughts and to take a moment to de-escalate from the day altogether.

On the ride, "Weak" by S.W.V. came on the radio. As soon as the song began to play, all sorts of memories instantly started to replay in Proof's mind.

September 2002

Proof and Scar were sitting in the car listening to Proof's favorite song, S.W.V. "Weak." If they could not agree on anything, they could always come together with music. Proof was sitting on Scar's lap singing to him, and he was taking in every note. Proof was always able to express herself through the lyrics of a song. Some things were just easier to say if she acted silly.

"Girl, don't play with me," Scar teased. Scar was attempting to control himself, but he had not seen Proof this happy in a while. Scar was about ten minutes from scooping Proof up and making her weak in the knees.

"What? I am just expressing myself," she flirted back. Proof and Scar were experiencing rough times lately. They had recently moved away from each other because they were evicted from their apartment, and the day and nights were becoming too long. Both Scar and Proof were immature in the area of money. Neither one understood the value of saving or budgeting. Scar wanted to please Proof; therefore, he never told her no, and Proof enjoyed shopping way too much. It seemed the more the song played, the deeper in love Proof became. It felt good to be with Scar without the drama.

"I love this CD! I feel S.W.V. made it just for us," Proof announced. Proof hated to tell Scar, but soon she was going to be leaving. The two shared a new baby, and she needed to get him home before too late, and she had work the next morning. Proof just scratched the surface of becoming a pharmacist and worked at the pharmacy in her neighborhood. Proof knew as soon as she told Scar she was leaving, the atmosphere would shift. For some reason lately, Scar desired her more than usual. It was cute at times but becoming hard to deal with. Scar just began to stare at Proof with a look of disbelief, admiring her beauty and charm.

Scar felt as if Proof was a dream that only comes true for someone else. His story and hers were different. Proof lived in the suburbs, and he lived in the streets. Proof was in undergrad, and Scar was barely working. Proof was always coming up with new adventures, and Scar just followed. However, that meant nothing to Proof. She loved Scar for who he was and nothing less. He took care of her in the best way he knew, and she was mesmerized with his street swagger. He was her bad boy, and she could not picture herself with anyone else. He was her Martin, and she was his Gina, but Scar continued to compare their differences and always convinced himself that he was not good enough. Proof glanced at the time to see it was getting late. She needed to leave; after all, she lived halfway across the city. She contemplated even saying anything, but the drive was long, and Proof was feeling herself getting tired. Proof was so looking forward to the day of them being under the same roof again.

"I have something for you," Scar said sweetly. From the beginning of their relationship, the two would always write letters or give cards to one another. Scar found it hard to verbally express his feelings, but writing always gave him the door needed for his genuine expressions.

"Awe, how sweet," Proof said. She enjoyed reading each and every letter or card that Scar wrote over and over. On those hard days of being without Scar, she would use them as a reminder of Scar's true feelings. She quickly opened the card to find the sweetest message from her husband.

My dearest Proof, thank you for being patient with me.

Oh great! Proof thought. This makes it even harder to tell Scar I need to go.

"Thank you, Scar. I will always remain patient with you but, Scar," she swallowed. "I am about to get the children and head on out," her voice quivering.

Instantly the dance that was in his eyes disappeared, and he immediately looked away. Proof could only imagine what was going through his mind. She attempted to grab his hand, but he pulled back before she could even touch him.

"I thought you were gonna spend the night?" Scar said quietly. Proof knew this was Scar's way of holding on to the moment, but she was not prepared for her and three children to be away from their typical living environment. She hated to put him through this goodbye, but her baby's comfort was foremost.

"Where am I going to sleep with three children, Scar?" She asked as sweetly as she knew how? She could tell in his eyes that Scar was slowly becoming someone else. Proof was becoming overwhelmed. What happened to her charmer? Where did he escape? All she could do was offer alternatives in hopes he would calm. "How about..." Scar interrupted before she could finish.

"You always do me like this. You always leave early," he scolded. She did not know what Scar was defining as early because it was almost midnight.

"Scar it has nothing to do with that, I am just trying to get the baby home before too late," she insisted. She wished he understood how much she wanted to stay. If she had it her way, she would never leave him. But someone had to be responsible for their children. It was not fair to have them uncomfortable because Scar and Proof wanted to lose themselves in one another all night.

"That baby is fine. You are just ready to go. You cannot go anywhere without your keys," and with that, he threw them into the back yard.

It was already late, and Proof had no idea how she was going to retrieve her keys. She had no choice but to ask for help. She went into the house without trying not to say too much and ask for help. As soon as Scar saw she got help, he began to come unhinged. Scar hated involving others in their affairs. He felt it was none of their concern, but, at this hour, what was Proof to do?

"Awe so you gonna involve my family?" he hollered. Proof was torn. She went from loving to loathing this man that was in front of her. Why did everything have to be so complicated? She and Scar had had such a beautiful night. Proof was growing angry because now Scar was acting like a child having a tantrum.

She tried to ignore him, but the more she did, the worse he got. Scar was not one to put his hands on Proof, but he could play a mean mind game. She was trying her best to retrieve the keys and leave. She could not move fast enough. She could feel Scar following her every move with his eyes. She knew that she would have to quickly leave without words or second thoughts as soon as she found them. *No goodbye kiss tonight,* she thought.

"I found them," she heard a voice say. *Thank God,* she thought. She could not retrieve them fast enough. Proof quickly grabbed her by standing children and got them strapped in to leave. She could feel Scar watching her every move. Deep inside, she knew tonight Scar was not going to be without his Proof.

As she was about to get into the car, Scar grabbed her and shouted, "You are not leaving without me." She had no choice but to allow him in the car, but where would they go? Her parents made it very clear that Scar was not allowed to stay over at their house, and she was in the car with three children, one of whom was an infant. Proof felt it was very selfish of Scar to prevent her and those children from going home.

"Scar, why are you doing this?" Proof begged.

"Because I need you tonight, and I don't want you to leave me," he said quietly. After sitting in the car for thirty minutes going back and forth, Proof got the idea to go to another family member's house that was in the area. Upon arrival, Proof went in to explain the situation while Scar went in to lay their children down safely. After speaking with Scar's cousin, she needed to take a couple of deep breaths to prepare for this night. God only knew what was going on in her husband's mind and Proof hated to admit that her beautiful night had ended in drama.

Scar was watching a television show when she walked into the room. At this point, Proof was exhausted and in much need of sleep. She had to be at work in about seven hours, but she was willing to talk with Scar and determine why he was so demanding of her company tonight.

"Scar, I'm here. What is going on?" she pleaded. Even this was too far out of character for Scar. He never wanted her to leave him, but he always gave in after a couple of minutes of persuasion and said his goodbyes.

"I can't just want the company of my wife? Damn!" Scar said, annoyed. Proof had had enough by this point. She was ready to abandon this night.

"Scar, I am about to go to sleep," she said.

"Why? I can't sleep!" he snapped. She knew that her Scar had left entirely, and she was dealing with a stranger. He grabbed her in a bear hug, refusing to let her go. Scar looked at her with tear-filled eyes. Immediately Proof's heart began to break. "Why do you want to leave me? You can't leave me like everyone else," Scar demanded. She decided to be quiet and allow him to talk. She honestly did not know what else to say or do.

Proof was startled from the phone ringing. "Hello," she said. Thoughts of her and Scar always do that. On the other end, the voice was saying sharply, "I have an order ready for a Proof Moings. Do you still need it?" Proof had forgotten her order entirely. *At some point, I have to turn Scar off in my mind*, she thought.

"Yes, I am on my way in," she said apologetically. It was hard to turn him off. That was the only way she could see or hear his voice. Each day grew harder without his familiar touch or embrace. Proof went in and retrieved her food and apologized for being late.

On the way home, she went back to her music, thinking about that night in September. That night was one night of unanswered questions. She never truly got to the bottom of his needs. She wanted to get the two of them to help through counseling. She wished that Scar would agree to talk to someone with her. However, she knew he would not, and she could not go alone. Scar had to be on board. What she saw in her husband that night was alarming. How could he change from charming to wreckless in a matter of seconds?

She remembered contacting his cousin and sharing her concerns, only for it to backfire in her face. His cousin thought the best solution would be to take all of Scar's notebooks of poems and letters and read them. He felt that was the only way to help by invading Scar's private thoughts. He felt the invasion would either prove or deny their worry of Scar being harmful to himself or others.

Proof had no idea that his notebooks were missing until one-day, Scar mentioned that he could not find his writings. She confronted his cousin, who admitted to taking them out of his backpack while he showered. Proof felt horrible about it. His cousin never even reported his findings. Thinking back on it now, it was the worst choice because, since that day, Scar never wrote to her again, not a poem, a card, or a letter. She had no idea how wounded and rejected that would leave his pride.

At that time in their marriage, Proof was so immature. She wished she would have understood then how she understands now. Her husband was yearning for her emotional support that night. Scar was just too prideful to admit it, and Proof was too underdeveloped to recognize it. God, at that very moment, allowed her to feel how Scar felt. Scar's only outlet had been ripped from him without warning. With tears in her eyes, she looked up and whispered, "That's why my marital business will always stay between Scar and me."

As soon as she got home and fed her children, she went into her closet and wrote this prayer.

Dear heavenly Father,

*Thank you for Your conviction in my heart. I honor an‹ praise You for all that you have ‹one for me. Lor‹, I repent in the name of Jesus for not taking my marital affairs to you but someone else. You are my **Jehovah Shalom**, my Lor‹ of peace. When I seek or‹er in my marriage, I will turn to You. I will trust in You with all my heart, leaning not to my un‹erstan‹ing an‹ knowing that You will ‹irect my path accor‹ing to your wor‹ in **Proverbs 3:5-6**. Thank You, Go‹, for forgiveness for not trusting in You but instea‹ putting my trust in man.*

It is so. In the name of Jesus, I pray.

Amen.

Proof hung the prayer along with all the others. She was so overwhelmed with emotions. She knew she needed to forgive herself; however, she could not allow this moment to pass without attempting to reach out to Scar. She reached for her phone, contemplating sending Scar a text message. She unlocked the phone and scrolled down to Scar's name. Proof began typing but quickly erased it. *Sending Scar a text will only crush my feelings; he will probably not respond*, she thought. Proof ended her prayer session, realizing that forgiveness for herself was the only way to heal. As she walked out of her private oasis, she quietly said, "Another long night in my bitterly cold reality."

4

Proverbs 24:3-4

Chapter 4

In your marital household, how do you title money? Yours or Ours?
"By wisdom, a house is built, and through understanding, it is estab-
lished; through knowledge, its rooms are filled with rare and beautiful
treasures." Proverbs 24:3-4

This week, instead of holding the marriage series on Sunday, the church decided to switch things up a bit and present on Friday night. Proof was slightly apprehensive because the church was labeling it *Date Night With a Twist*. This service meant that she had to prepare herself for the many couples who would show up and the various games and questions that would be played throughout the night. She decided not to attend; however, God always provided her a ram in the bush. One of the ladies who taught a life group with Proof asked if she would go with her. Her husband worked often, and she didn't want to go alone. Proof did not know how she knew Scar was not going, but she was glad she would not miss out. The plan was for the couples to have dinner before the series began and then meet at church. Her friend was so elated that Proof had agreed to come with her, she insisted on providing dinner for the both of them. Proof made her way through the crowd to find her friend sitting alone, waiting patiently on her.

"Hey, beautiful. I tried to get your sandwich the way you like it," she smiled. Her friend possessed one of the sweetest spirits. She was always willing to go out of her way to please others, and Proof welcomed her kindness.

"You are fine. I am just glad to have the company," Proof assured. Proof would have given anything to have Scar by her side, but she appreciated this moment with her friend. As she sat and ate, she became distracted by the numerous couples interacting with one another. Many were eating dinner, but some were just sitting and talking, which Proof dearly missed regarding her union with Scar.

"Girl, my husband does not do these types of things, so he was glad I had someone else to go with," said her friend. Proof just laughed and agreed. Deep down inside, Proof wanted to cry, but God knew what He was doing.

It was challenging for Proof to be in situations such as these. Of course, she was excited for all the happy couples, but Scar's absence was more relative in arenas such as this. Proof was forced to face her reality face to face.

"Girl let me call my husband and make sure he has the clothes he needs for the night," her friend said. She hurried off to make her call. The thought crossed over Proof's mind to reach out to Scar. She wanted to call him, but what if he did not answer? She tried at least twice a week to either text or call him, but he never responded. She felt so empty and defeated each time. She said a small prayer and dialed his number. To her amazement, he answered.

"Hello," he said. Proof's heart dropped into her lap. The sound of his voice echoed so profoundly within her spirit. Her mind instantly came up with a million conversation starters. Where have you been? Why do you always ignore my calls? Are you coming home soon?

"Hey, love," she said, shocking herself. Proof decided that bombarding him with questions would only give him an excuse to dismiss her. The time had grown too long since she last heard his voice. God would allow them time for her to have answers to her questions, but she would just enjoy the moment for now.

"What's up? I'm at work." Scar scolded. Proof knew that was his excuse when he did not want to talk long. He would always answer when he was too busy to talk, Scar knew how much Proof hated it, but at this point, she was just glad to hear his voice.

"What da hell is all that noise?" Scar demanded. Proof could recognize irritation in his voice. She sadly knew that this conversation was not going to be productive or long.

"I am at a marriage conference," Proof said. She was secretly hoping that would spark a conversation, but she sadly knew it would not by his dismissive demeanor.

"You at a what? Why are you at that?" he asked, confused. Proof could only imagine his thoughts. Scar was never one to do conferences. He looked at them as a form of professional counseling. He never came to realize that they were an actual aid for Proof and a much-needed investment into their union.

"Just getting some pointers. Maybe being here will assist me in getting you back home," Proof joked. She was making light of the situation, but she prayed that it would. Being without Scar was growing more challenging daily. Coming to an empty home and bed nightly was more damaging than one could imagine.

"Maybe not," Scar replied. Scar at times could respond in the rudest manners. However, Proof recognized this as a protective shell he created to prevent himself from Proof's repeated rejection.

"Why do you say that, Scar?" Proof asked. Proof knew the answer, but she felt the longer she could keep the conversation, the longer she could remain in Scar's presence.

"There you go, Proof. I am at work. I'll call you back later," Scar said, annoyed. Proof knew that it would be another six weeks or longer before she spoke with him again as soon as she said goodbye.

Scar was beginning to distance himself, and Proof could recognize the change. When he first left, he and Proof talked often. They created pacific times for conversation, but as time expanded, their conversation dissipated. Only God could reveal why Scar chose to distance himself.

"Alright, then. I love you, Scar. Enjoy your night at work," she said in bitterness. Saying goodbye became more difficult each time. Scar and Proof used to battle over who would hang up first. She longed for those days to return.

"I love you too, Proof. Bye," Scar replied sharply. Something about how he sounded made Proof worry, but Scar would never share from fear of her sharing with others. Proof could feel the tears welling up in her eyes, but she cut them off as soon as she saw her friend coming. Proof was not about to allow her friend to see her nakedness. She did not have time for empty promises, ones that are made only to appease the moment.

"Girl, my husband is so silly. He told me to make sure I get some clues on what to wear on our date night," her friend teased. Proof laughed, attempting her best to hold back tears, wishing her conversation had gone that smoothly. "Let's get in here before we don't have a seat," joked her friend.

Proof could not understand why the crowd was so massive and thick. It was just a Friday night service. When they walked through the doors, the fellowship hall had been turned into a dance floor, and love ballads played encouraging couples to get up and dance with one another. Proof and her friend both looked at each other and said, "can I have this dance?" It was apparent that both of them were uncomfortable, and evident both were considering the option of leaving.

"There is no need to leave now; we are already here," suggested Proof. They both slid into a spot at a back table in hopes of not looking suspicious. A man came on the mic to welcome all the couples and ask them to have a seat to begin. *Thank God*, Proof thought. They must have had the dance before the series started. The man greeted everyone and introduced the night topic: *In your martial household, how do you title money? Yours or Ours?* They had the cutest skit of a couple struggling with how to divide their money. The wife made more than the man, and she had a shopping problem. She had always been told if a man does not spoil his wife, he doesn't love her. Her money is her money, and his money is her money. This began to ring too many bells for Proof. She had always been career-driven. Proof worked from the age of 17 and always supported herself. However, she was never taught how to save or budget, and she had a shopping problem as well. Scar hated it, and he complained about it all the time. Proof would go and buy things and then hide them in her closet as if she had them all along. Scar would get mad about it. Then he would go for weeks without talking to her. Proof's mind began to wander off as the skit continued.

January 2005

"Are you serious, Scar?" asked Proof. She could not believe what she was hearing. Scar was about to do something that showed just how much he trusted and loved Proof.

"Do I play?" Scar questioned. The two were on their way to the naval bank to sign paperwork making Proof power of attorney over Scar. At the time, Scar was in the Marines and was being deployed to Iraq. Scar knew he needed to do more to provide for his family; therefore becoming active in the military made sense.

The world was finally beginning to look bright for the Moings family. Scar was excited that he was given this vital opportunity to support his family. Until now, it had always been Proof. He was more than happy to hand over power to his Queen.

"If something happens to me while I am gone, I need to know that my children and wife are going to be well taken care of," said Scar.

"Understandable," replied Proof. She did not want to think about something happening to Scar, but this was the reality of being a military wife.

"How can I help you, sir?" asked the teller. Scar stood proudly, holding on to his son. Proof stood back, admiring his courageousness.

"I am leaving for Iraq, and I want to make my wife a power of attorney over my stuff," Scar said proudly. Proof could not help but smile. She was so honored that Scar was choosing her for something of this importance.

"Of course, sir, I'll be glad to assist," responded the teller. "It sounds like you need a General P.O.A.," the teller stated. "This gives your wife the power to be your voice in your absence. This type of P.O.A. is vast, sir. You can set a time frame on it, or you can leave it in place until you return," the teller informed.

As Proof was listening, she had no idea what this all involved. *If Scar is willing to give me P.O.A., I need to take it very seriously*, Proof thought. The woman continued to explain how Proof would have access to all of Scar's personal matters and that this privilege would not be taken lightly. She looked at Scar and received the final word to authorize the P.O.A., and with a few signatures, it was complete.

Scar and Proof decided to take their family out for dinner because moments like this would not happen in a few weeks. To see Scar making boss moves excited Proof. She was so proud of her man. He had always been willing to take care of her and make sure she kept a beautiful smile on her face.

As they were eating dinner, Scar began to look at Proof in that unique way again. She just looked at him and smiled because she knew all too well what that look meant. In the past, it irritated Proof to have Scar stare at her, but soon she realized it was his way of absorbing himself in her existence.

"Proof, I trust you, I hope you know that. I am giving you P.O.A. because I know you will handle my affairs correctly. Do not spend all my money on clothes," he scolded. He laughed afterward; however, Scar was quite serious. He had heard all too often how men would travel to Iraq only to come home to wives who had either cheated, divorced, or spent all of their money on lavish things, and he did not need that from Proof. Proof looked at Scar with complete sureness in her eyes, understanding that being careless with this responsibility would change the dynamic of their relationship forever.

"I would never do that," guaranteed Proof. The family finished their meal and left the restaurant. Proof was overly eager to make it home and show her king how much his actions were genuinely significant for her on this day.

April 2005

Scar had been gone from Proof for about three months now, and she missed him more than words could express. She forgot how warm his body was as he laid beside her, how his lips felt as he woke her when he would return home from work, and most importantly, him doing the little things like bringing in the groceries, helping her put them up, or putting things together around the house. She had already received two of his payroll checks, and instead of putting them up like instructed, she spent them on eating out, clothes, and nights out with friends. She knew it was wrong, but she missed Scar, and this was how she coped with him being gone. Her friends at work told her she was crazy and dumb, but she just stopped sharing with them. They did not understand anyway. Their husbands were at home every night, plus she was going to put it all back. She just wanted the kids not to miss their daddy, and this way, they wouldn't, so she thought.

Proof must have been staring off for too long because she could feel her friend nudging her in the back. "Girl, where did you go?" her friend questioned.

"Far away from here," Proof teased. The man with the mic encouraged the couples to write down times that they hid money or were not honest about how much they had spent on something. Proof immediately went back to her thoughts. Still, to this day, the thoughts of being careless with such an important task wrecked her soul.

"We can do ours together, Proof," said her friend. Proof immediately wrote about spending all of Scar's money while he was away in Iraq. She felt that sharing may allow the door to open for release and forgiveness for herself.

"Girl, that is crazy. You took all that man's money." Scolded her friend. The look of shock on her friend's face was immense. Proof could only imagine her thoughts. Proof quickly realized that she made the wrong choice to share.

"Well, not all of it. I rented an apartment, bought furniture, and a game that Scar wanted," Proof responded. Proof was still attempting to make excuses for something she knew was unacceptable.

"Girl, it's a wonder y'all are still together. Most men don't come back from that," her friend said—another reason why Proof never shared. Of course, when her friend shared, it was some ridiculousness about her husband giving her a $100 bill once, and she bought something for $3.25 and kept the change. Proof wanted to say, "girl take several seats!" and as her students said, "Miss me with that bull $ %#@."

This was not the arena for Proof. She needed to find an excuse to leave. She had heard and seen enough. Plus, unlike the others in the room, she had to drive home alone and be willing to care for her children's nightly needs alone.

"Girl, I think I am about to head out. It's getting late, and unlike these other brides, I have to drive myself home," Proof exclaimed. It was apparent Proof had become exasperated with this night of love.

"I think I will go too; I have the same situation," joked her friend. Proof could feel her side-eye game approaching. *Really! Your husband will be home soon*, Proof thought. On the way, home Proof returned to her earlier thoughts. The sound of anger in Scar's voice would never be forgotten when he discovered what Proof had done with the money he left her. To this day, she would still get chills from what she has now termed the *Iraq Scandal*.

November 2006

"Proof! Why do you have all these receipts?" questioned Scar. Proof was good at hiding things; however, she kept every receipt in her closet box. This was something her mother taught her years ago. "Keep up with all of your receipts, just in case you have to take something back," her mother would say. Unfortunately, that had backfired this time. While she was at work, Scar went through all of Proof's things and found out what she had been buying in his absence. Proof tried to turn it around on him. "Why are you going through my things, Scar?" Proof snapped back.

"To find out what da hell you were doing while I was gone," Scar scolded back. "I was out here fighting a war for this damn country, and my fucking wife was at home spending my damn money on lunch for some damn body else!" shouted Scar.

Scar was mad as hell, and there was nothing Proof could do but come clean. He had all the receipts in his hands. Proof attempted to grab Scar and hug him, but he just pushed her off.

"Don't try that shit with me. I told your ass when I was gone not to spend my money on shit. What da fuck did you do with your check? You ate that shit too?" Scar shouted.

Proof had never seen Scar like this before. She could always calm him, but this time, Scar could not stand her sight. Proof had never been this afraid of Scar. Her first thought was, *why did you not throw those receipts away Proof? Next, she went to how stupid of an idea it was to disappoint Scar.* Then her thoughts went to pure regret because now her marriage was over. She knew Scar was never going to forgive her.

"I am sorry, baby. I missed you, so I took the kids out and some of my friends too," Proof pleaded. "I was trying to not think about how much I missed you," Proof continued. Proof was searching for anything to calm Scar. She did not like the beast he was transforming into. Where did her loving husband go?

"What the fuck ever. You took your ass and spent my money and yours, and now we have no fucking savings. I was in Iraq getting shot at daily, and you were at home wining and dining others nightly," Scar shouted.

He picked Proof up and threw her on the ground. All Proof could see was the bottom of Scars boot. Her heart was beating so fast. Scar had never put his hands on her, and she could not come to grips with this sudden beastly change. Suddenly, Scar halted, looked at Proof, and walked out the room to the couch. He did not talk to Proof for weeks after. He only would stare and remain silent.

Proof made it home, and the lights from her beautiful house made her heart hurt worse. Why was her husband not in the car with her? Why was he not at least on the porch waiting for her? She turned off the ignition and got ready to go in. That time in November was the beginning of their downfall. Soon after Scar's discovery, Proof and Scar separated. Scar could not take Proof's dishonesty. Proof grew angry at herself all over again. Why did she spend Scar's money? Where would they have been now if she hadn't? She wished she could go back; she would have done it all differently. She decided before she went in for the night that she would write a prayer to speak over herself for healing for their future finances together, because of course, now Scar did not trust her with money.

Dear Heavenly Father,

*Thank You as always for your presence. Your mercies are new every morning, an• for that, I am grateful. Lor•, in the past, I have been that foolish wife that you speak of in **Proverbs 14**. I am repenting now, Go•, an• asking You to create in me the wis•om nee•e• to be the wife that rebuil•s my house on Your foun•ation. Lor•, You are my **Jehovah- Rophe**, my healer. Thank you, Lor•, that Scar will begin to trust in You, so he will begin to lea• our family strongly with Your grace. Thank you, Lor•, for •aily recreation. For you are creating me into the virtuous woman, you i•entify in **Proverbs 31**. I have faith in Your wor•, Go•. Thank You for Your Will be •one in my life.*

It is so. In Jesus's name, I pray.

Amen.

Proof looked in the mirror to check her face for any evidence of tears or stress. When she entered the house, she knew her children would bombard her daily worries and activities. Proof understood the importance of shifting gears. However, nights like this made it difficult for Proof to transform from hurt and lonely wife to a loving and caring mother. It was these nights that gave her children short answers and quick bedtimes. She learned how to hide her feelings rather quickly, but she never learned how to shake her emotions. With her new prayer clinched in her hands, she gathered her things and made her way into her house to finish the night with her babies.

5

Hebrews 13:4

Chapter 5

Give honor to marriage, and remain faithful to one another in marriage. God will surely judge people who are immoral and those who commit adultery. Hebrews 13:4

January 2007

The past months for Proof and Scar were grim. Scar paid no attention to Proof. He moved around their home as if she had no existence in his life. Proof attempted several times to communicate with Scar, but he either gave her a glare of unacceptance or ignored her presence. Coming home for Proof grew very uncomfortable. Walking in knowing her husband was not going to acknowledge her was torture. Proof had run out of ideas to reconcile with Scar. She recognized that what she did was very wrong and selfish, but Proof could not take Scar acting as if she did not exist. Proof decided the best move was to give Scar an ultimatum, she and Scar needed to separate for a moment to heal.

"Scar, I know I am not your favorite, but can we talk?" Proof nervously said. She prayed that Scar would at least nod his head or something. It was apparent she was standing there, and he could hear her.

"What the hell for?" Scar snapped. The sight of Proof made his blood boil. If she had any awareness of what he had just experienced in Iraq, she would have been slightly as agitated as him.

"I am only asking Scar because I hate what we have become," Proof insisted. All she wanted was to crack the ice slightly. She was exhausted by the elephant in the room that kept her company.

"You hate what we have become?" Scar said in shock. Scar was trying his hardest to remain calm. He knew that his children were in the house, and they were his only therapy currently. Truthfully they were the only reason Scar woke up daily to even deal with Proof.

Proof was running low on conversation starters. Therefore, she just blurted out... "Look, Scar, we have to talk about our future. Are we going to be married or not?"? Scar had Proof up against a wall. She understood the risk that she was taking, but she had to get an answer, no matter how hard it was to receive.

"Well, Proof, the next day our children go to your mother's house, we will talk then," Scar said. Scar was not willing to have a conversation of this magnitude with his children in arms reach.

Proof said no words, and she just responded with a nod of her head. At this point, she would take any form of communication from Scar. Until this moment, their only interaction was awkward and cold. Proof quickly ran to confirm arrangements with her mother to keep their children. She wanted to hurry before he changed his mind.

Proof woke up with a profuse amount of sweat. Dreaming about the "Iraq Scandal" brought back uncomfortable memories that she preferred to remain buried. Proof needed to get up so that she could prepare herself for a weekend free of children. She had not had a moment without everyone away from the house in months. Since the departure of Scar, she felt it necessary to keep her partial family together. As she grew wiser, she understood the importance of being involved with her children and their moments. With Scar gone, she made a personal pact with herself that one parent needed to be there for their children.

All of her children were dispersed throughout the city safely. Proof had planned a day of meditation with a good run, food, and God. The previous night's service *Date Night With a Twist* was a bit excessive. Proof was triggered in a way she had not been in a while. Mainly because she could not shake these thoughts of Scar; of course, he was her husband, and he should be on her mind and heart, but today he was weighing on her heart differently. She realized that Scar answering her call twice in one week would be a miracle, but she got the courage to attempt it anyway.

She grabbed her phone, scrolled down to his name, and pressed the green phone button before she could come up with a second alternative. "Hello," Scar answered. Proof's mind was blown. She took a deep breath, knowing she needed to be quick and to the point.

"Scar, I just wanted to hear your voice," she said. Proof had learned that dancing around the issue with Scar only irritated him. She realized long ago to spit it out. Besides, she wanted him to feel he was needed. Plus, the sound of his voice was always serene to her. Scar had not been this cold since he discovered she spent his money in the *Iraq Scandal*, which was a tricky time in their marriage.

"Well, you hear it. What's up, Proof?" Scar scolded. Scar sounded empty. The serene tone of his voice was fading. Proof felt the warmth of tears coming to her eyes. *Why is my husband attempting to detach from me?* She wondered. She thought it best to end the conversation now before it damaged her soul any deeper.

"I truly love you, Scar, and I just wanted you to hear me say it," Proof said quietly. "Enjoy whatever this day brings you, Scar," she added. With that, she hung up the phone to begin her day of meditation.

The day was more than beautiful as Proof prepared for her morning run. She decided that since she did not have children's worries at home, she would run six miles instead of her usual five. As always, the smell of the air was so refreshing to her spirit. Today more than anything, Proof needed this run. As the pavement hit her shoes, and she began to focus on her stride, her mind returned to the *Iraq Scandal's*.

January 2007

Proof returned from dropping off their children with her mother. Scar was nowhere to be found. Proof began to entertain the idea of growing a deeper relationship with God. She believed in prayer but never really applied it to her life. It was just a mere ritual; go to church because it was Sunday. But a group of new friends began to introduce Proof to a new faith practice. Her friends would meet weekly, encouraging one another in God by reading scriptures and praying. Proof saw so many positive changes in her friends, and it was impressive. Proof decided to attend a church service with them, plus she welcomed the outlet.

She and Scar did not go out at all anymore. Since his return and her scandal, they had begun just to coexist. During the service, the pastor suggested the idea of fasting for God to answer a prayer request. Proof needed her prayers to be answered concerning Scar. The death silence had to leave her home. Scar's recent dealings with Proof began to grow extreme. Therefore, Proof decided to fast for this night. She wanted their conversation to go well, and she wanted them both to get up with answers.

Proof had not eaten all day, and it was almost six o'clock, and Scar was nowhere in sight. Proof's stomach was over the fast as well. *What is the purpose anyway? Scar loathe* her *an* woul* most likely always feel that way*, She thought. As she made her way to grab something quick from the kitchen, Scar appeared suddenly walking down the stairs. He had been there the whole time. She assumed he was either upstairs and did not hear her or was still ignoring her presence.

"Hey, Scar!" Proof said in shock. Proof thought she would wait to eat. After all, God must be moving. She was afraid if she ate, she may taint their conversation.

"Hey, Proof," Scar said, smiling. Proof could not believe it Scar had not smiled at her in months. His smile looked genuine and almost made Proof run and embrace him. "Did the children do okay when you dropped them off?" he asked.

"Of course, you know my mother is the only place they want to be," Proof said. "If they could, they would trade us in for her," Proof joked. She was joking, but she knew their children felt the tension from her and Scar as well.

"Well, Proof, what are we gonna do?" Scar asked. Proof was shocked. Scar was just jumping right in. She was not expecting him to be so forward. She thought she would have to dance around the issue a bit.

"Honestly, Scar, I understand that I have hurt you and maybe beyond repair, but I feel we should take a moment apart and see what happens," Proof suggested. Proof was attempting to answer the thoughts that might have been in Scar's mind all these weeks.

"Well, if that is what you want Proof, okay," Scar said, looking shocked. He had no idea that was what she was going to say. He thought they would come to a solution, but he was determined not to have the drama, so he agreed.

"It is not what I want, Scar, I feel it is what we need. I am confused about how someone can walk around for months and not communicate with someone they claim to love," Proof stated. Scar had done things in their past that hurt Proof, but she would have never totally wiped him away as Scar had her.

"Proof you hurt me. I would never take your money and use it the way you did mine," Scar stated. It was obvious he was deeply hurt by the actions of his wife. "But, Proof, I am not going to fight you," Scar said. *Maybe ·eep ·own, we genuinely nee· a break*, Scar thought.

"I cannot change what I did, Scar. I need you to forgive me, and I feel that you either do not want to or cannot," Proof stated. Proof found it challenging to wrap her head around more weeks with Scar and her living in silence. She was making suggestions out of her pain. She felt it was not a wise choice, but she could not think of any other peaceful options.

After a long night, she and Scar reluctantly decided that a temporary separation was needed. Over the next week, they both worked to separate their marital life. Neither was happy with the choice, but neither was willing to speak up.

April 2007

Proof was beginning to become very close with her new group of supportive friends; they were distracting her from the reality of Scar leaving. Over time they began meeting more often. The weekly meetings were not enough for the type of support Proof needed. Being in the company of others was a much-needed therapy. Veto, one of the young men in the group, decided to come over and assist with moving some oversized items back into place. The two began to grow very close, and he responded well to her children. Proof enjoyed their conversations about goals and life. They talked almost every day for hours upon hours. Their conversations reminded Proof of how she and Scar were at the beginning of their relationship.

Proof did not want to admit her feelings, but she had begun to grow very fond of Veto. She knew that her feelings were inappropriate and they should not be entertained; however, she continued their talks and interactions.

Veto was not Scar, but he was the option for now. His interest in Proof was complementary. Veto gave Proof his undivided attention; he never made her feel not welcomed or displaced. Their attraction for one another became evident and grew harder to ignore. After several secret meetings between the two, they eventually entered into forbidden territory.

Something inside Proof begged her to end this new romance, but the attention Veto offered was not something Proof wanted to stop. Proof felt the need, however, to establish boundaries with Veto. She was unwilling to allow him into territory that belonged only to Scar; therefore, their heated season only involved affectionate kissing and long hugs. The others in the prayer group noticed the apparent shift in their relationship as well. None would confirm their suspicions, but

Proof would have friends come and offer their opinions about her forbidden lover.

One night the group decided to attend an all-night prayer service. Proof was excited to participate in. God's word was always a form of healing, and recently she had begun to feel an unshakeable shame. During the service, Proof's soul was repeatedly convicted. She became very emotional. Veto attempted to reach out and comfort her as always, but this time his touch made her flinch. It was almost instantly; his touch felt like prickly thorns all over her body. Proof could not explain it. At that moment, she yearned for Scar more than she had ever before. Proof found herself running toward the altar for prayer.

A lady was standing at the altar, and Proof ran straight into her arms. Proof didn't have to say much the lady immediately began to pray calling out everything that Veto and Proof had been involved in. Proof could feel shame and regret exiting her body like a train. Proof tried to pull away from the women, but she would not let her go. She just continued with her prayers.

Once the woman finished, Proof got up and stumbled back to her seat, attempting her hardest to ignore Veto. After the service, the group decided to go to breakfast. At breakfast, Proof called Veto to the side and ended their forbidden love. She knew that God was giving her a warning, and she needed to take heed.

Proof could feel her heart almost pounded out of her chest. She felt a sense of regret all over again. Proof remembered after that night, she called Scar and told him everything. She went through a phase of not being settled in her spirit; she could not sleep nor had an appetite. She vowed to herself that, after that, no matter what choices. Scar made. She was not going to escape their relationship with another again.

Proof could see her house in the distance, and unlike other days, she was ready for this run to end. She was overly excited for her shower and prayer time. She did not know how God would restore her broken family, but she knew deep inside that he would. She felt that she and Scar held a bond that could not be easily broken. Deep inside, she knew that if Scar truly wanted to be out of her life, he would have ended communication with her a long time ago. Proof ended her run, wiped her face, and got ready to begin her day of peace knowing her babies were safe, and God was working it all out behind the scenes.

Dear Heavenly Father,

I am coming before you with a broken heart an▪ spirit. I know that I have allowe▪ myself to become involve▪ with another. I am asking for forgiveness an▪ restoration of my heart. Lor▪, please ▪eliver me from the ▪esire of my forbi▪ ▪en lover. My only passion is for my husban▪, an▪ I am sorry for attempting to fill that broken place with another. Thank you for instant conviction in the future if my soul shall ever won▪er again.

It is so. In Jesus's name, I pray.

Amen.

6

Corinthians 6:14

Chapter 6

As a couple, do you pray and read the Bible together regularly?
"Be ye not unequally yoked together with unbelievers: for what fellow-
ship hath righteousness with unrighteousness? What communion hath
light with darkness?" 2 Corinthians 6:14

June 2008

Proof was on her way to a divorce attorney. She and Scar did not see eye to eye on anything. All they did was fight. Proof had had enough. She felt that their best years were past them. One of her friends had given her all the information needed to get it done for free. "Are there any kids involved?" the pro bono attorney asked.

Proof replied, "Yes, we have three children." Her three children were the only glue that was holding her and Scar together. However, that was not enough any longer. Proof and Scar attempted to amend after the *Iraq Scan•al*, but their bond's tenderness had not returned.

"Is there going to be a hassle over them? If so, you cannot come through us. Having a struggle would mean it is a contested divorce, which we do not handle," she informed Proof. Proof could not believe that she was actually in this office answering these questions. It felt rushed but needed.

"No, this will not be contested," Proof assured. One thing about Proof was that she would never keep Scar's children from him. The attorney informed Proof of the process. One had to have a divorce case pending for three months before finalizing in her state. After that, both parties would come to court and speak before a judge either denied or approved the case. If approved, once she left the court, she would be a divorced woman. Proof assured the lady she understood and retrieved the papers from her to be signed by Mr. Scar Moings.

Proof left the court immediately on her way to Scar. She jumped out of the car with all power in her hands, so she thought. For the first time, this was not a threat. She was truly ready to go through with it. She and Scar would no longer be Scar and Proof. She walked up on the porch feeling like a brand new woman. Scar had been sitting there waiting.

"You cute today, Proof," he teased. Seeing Proof always gave Scar indescribable joy. Scar would admit that their union was different, but it was their union and he loved his wife.

"You must be looking," she responded. Proof had been on a severe workout grind, and her figure never looked better, especially being a mother of three. Exercising was the priceless therapy she needed.

"Look, Scar, I am not going to stay long, but I need you to sign these," as she pushed the papers toward his way. Proof knew there was going to be a disagreement about it. Therefore, she was ready to begin it so it could end.

"What da hell is this?" Scar questioned. Scar informed Proof at the beginning of their union that divorce would not be an option. He treasured their marriage, and no matter the issues, he desired it to remain intact.

"I went to a divorce lawyer today Scar. This is not working any longer. All we do is argue constantly, and I don't know about you, but I want better for us. Plus, I have been with you since the 10th grade, and I need to explore new options," Proof informed. Scar was all Proof ever new besides Veto, and she wanted to explore more options, but, this time, she wanted to do it correctly.

"Girl shut da hell up! You are not leaving me, and I am not leaving you. We are just having a hard time right now, but we will make it through like we always do," Scar assured. Scar was unbothered by her pleas. As far as he was concerned, Proof was just whining like usual.

"Not this time, Scar. You will not keep a steady job. I don't know how many new women are on the side, and to be honest, I am simply exhausted!" Proof exclaimed. Proof felt she was no longer enough. She felt there was always some woman ready to remind Scar of what she was not.

"Proof I am not signing those papers, and that's that on that," as he attempted to pull her down on his lap. Scar would always overlook Proof's truth. It seemed he would not take the opportunity to speak with her and truly hear her concerns.

"Scar, when was the last time you ate?" Proof questioned. Proof knew if she got him to focus on something else, he would open to her wants.

"Yesterday," he answered. The absence of Proof gave Scar no reason to care. He would eat when it was absolutely necessary; otherwise, he just existed.

"If I buy you some food now, will you sign then?" Proof asked. *Bingo*, she thought.

"I'll sign, but we not getting a divorce. I will assure you on that, " he said with a solemn look.

Scar signed, and Proof quickly grabbed them from his hands just in case he would renege and rip them up. She could not believe that it was over. She honored her word and got him something to eat. Her marriage was about to end on a sack full of Krystal's cheeseburgers.

July 2008

Proof was getting ready for church. She was so excited to attend this new church. She was growing spiritually; God had been indeed showing up in her life. It seemed every Sunday; God presented a message for her spoken through the voice of the pastor. She could hear her phone ringing, but whoever it was would have to call back. This was her worshiping hour. The phone continued to sound a persistent ring that would not stop. She finally answered.

"Hello," sounding annoyed. Whoever it was had better make it quick. She did not want to interrupt her praise for too long.

"Good morning, beautiful," Scar's voice smiling. Proof was not in the mood. Scar needed to speak fast and quickly. She only had about 30 more minutes before a child came in and needed her.

"What you want, boy? I'm in the middle of my praise," Proof answered. Proof could only imagine what he needed.

"I just wanted to speak to my beautiful wife this morning," Scar replied. One thing about Scar was his charm. It was something Proof could never avoid, and Scar knew it.

"What's up, Scar?" she responded. He had her attention now. She was eager to see what this interruption was all about. Why was Scar so persistent?

"I was wondering if you were willing to come to church with me today," Scar suggested.

"Are you serious, Scar? You go to church now?" she teased. Proof was shocked. Church was always her suggestion. Scar was never willing to attend.

"I do, and I would love for you and the children to come to church with me today," insisted Scar. Scar began to miss Proof more each day, and he was willing to adjust to win his Queen back.

"I was going to go to my own church, Scar." Proof enjoyed the spiritual atmosphere at her church. Whenever she attended, she was always lifted and inspired to continue toward whatever God had for her.

"I know, but you can miss one Sunday." Scar was determined to be with his family today, and he needed Proof's corporation with his offer. Something about being in the presence of the Lord made Scar thirst for his family.

Proof could not believe she was on her way to Scar's church. This man never was disrespectful to God, but he was definitely not a consistent churchgoer. He would always make an excuse: it's football Sunday,

I was out drinking all night. "Say a prayer for me," he would holler as she walked out the door, but he never would go. *God must be truly working on Scar's heart*, Proof thought.

As she pulled in the church parking lot, Scar was outside waiting for her. He rushed to her car and gave her the most significant embrace. Proof attempted to act as if she could care less, but his embrace felt so familiar and warm; she honestly did not want to let go. Proof had not felt Scar like this in years. He grabbed the children and whisked all of them into the church.

The church was so pleasant and comfortable. Proof could feel God's presence upon entry. She tried to tell herself don't get caught up, but she could not stop the feelings that were bubbling up on the inside. Scar already had seats saved for them, and as soon as they took their seats, he took Proof by the hand and whispered into her ear, "Thanks for coming. You look beautiful." Proof was lost and did not want to move from that moment. She wished she could pause time right there at that moment.

Proof honestly did not remember much about church service. All she remembered was how warm Scar was the entire service. Scar introduced her and the kids to everyone after church, and it made Proof feel so important and valued. This is what she had been praying for so long. She was speechless.

"You want to go to dinner with my family today?" Scar suggested. Proof and Scar's family had always been close. She loved them as much as they loved her. She could spend hours upon hours with them, but she did not want to give Scar the wrong impression. The divorce had one more month left, and she would not have him think she would not go through with it. She was determined to end this union and excited to begin to look toward new opportunities.

"Okay, Scar as friends I will attend, but understand our divorce is still pending," Proof reminded. After a day like this, she did not trust herself with his charm. She did not need to get caught up with sudden changes from Scar.

"Proof just enjoy the day; you are worried about the wrong thing," Scar scolded.

Dinner, as usual, was delicious. His family had some fabulous cooks and even better conversation. Proof had been laying low in fear of Scar getting the wrong impression of her plans. This was the first time she and the children had been around them in quite some time. She loved every moment. Every once in a while, she glanced up and noticed Scar staring at her that unique way he always did. Her attempts to ignore him were getting weaker by the second. It was getting late, and she needed to leave, but she was very hesitant in fear of waking up from this dream of a day.

Scar walked up to Proof and wrapped his hands around her waist and kissed her neck, "You about ready to leave?" The way his voice echoed in her spirit made her heart skip a thousand beets. She wanted to scream no loudly, but instead, she swallowed hard and responded, "it is about that time."

The day was picture perfect, filled with love and compassion, plus their children loved being with their father all day. Proof understood this day was more priceless to more than her. Proof's children were a main motivation for her to stay.

She grabbed the children, and Scar helped her out of the house and to her car. He kissed each of the kids, and when he got to Proof, he looked into her big brown eyes and said, "Thanks again for coming to church with me today. I enjoyed my family. Maybe you can come back next Sunday," and with those words, he kissed her on both cheeks, her forehead, and finally her lips. Proof was so overwhelmed she almost dissolved in Scar's arms, but she refused to let him see. Her attempts to play hard were getting weaker by the minute, and Scar was well aware.

"You're right, Scar, it was good for the children to see you in church. They can spend the weekend with you next week and go to church with you on Sunday. That way, I can get a break," Proof announced.

It would be at least two more Sundays before Proof returned with Scar and as she predicted his charm grew harder to ignore. Proof began wrestling with the idea of leaving her church and going with Scar. Currently, she loved her church and the growth she was encountering spiritually, but she and Scar were beginning to read the bible and pray more often together.

After devotion on Wednesday night, her pastor got up announcing that if anyone was struggling with the idea of leaving and attending another church with their spouse, please follow. Proof felt he was talking directly to her. At the end of the devotion, she got up and began her quest toward her new church.

Late August 2008

Proof never really told Scar that she would change her membership; she just allowed him to lead and began coming each Sunday. She began to enjoy this family time. Scar had become the husband that she had been praying for.

One Sunday during service, the pastor asked if anyone in the congregation wanted to join. Before Proof knew it, Scar grabbed her hand and stood up. She was outdone. God was replacing the order within her home. He was aligning their family in His order and not the world's demand. Not only did Scar commit to joining the church, but he also stated that he wanted to be baptized.

After church, the first lady of the church came over to Proof and began talking with her. She and Proof had spoken before, but this time Proof could tell she had something on her heart that needed to be said.

"Are you still going through with your divorce?" she asked. She was very forward, and it threw Proof off. *Is it really any of your concern,* she thought. However, Proof was not going to be impolite.

"I am," Proof responded. Proof was confused as to why everyone was so concerned about what she and Scar were doing. People get divorced daily. Why were Scar and Proof such a big deal?

"God is going to make a way that you will not divorce Scar, and not only that, you will have at least two more children," she calmly said.

Okay, now she has gone too far. Proof and Scar were satisfactory. They were building a healthy friendship and were working well co-parenting with one another. However, the thought of a happily ever after with Scar was not a current prayer for Proof.

"You may have the wrong individual; my marriage has been over for some time," Proof assured. Proof believed in the move of God, but God knew Proof's desire. She wondered what her first lady saw that she was obviously missing from her sight.

"God brought you here for a reason. Those divorce papers were shredded the moment you hit that door. Just admit it, Proof, Scar makes you happy. Can you make it without him?" She insisted. Her conversation was beginning to wear Proof down. She was starting to rethink her motives behind her divorce. This conversation was actually beginning to make Proof uncomfortable.

"Scar only brings about 5% to the table. Looks can be deceiving. Scar still has a lot of work to do," Proof said, annoyed. Proof was hoping that this would make her back off of her and move one. Proof was not trying to be rude, but her persistence made Proof feel emotions that she had attempted to bury.

With the most sincere look on her face, she said to Proof, "But all that being said, can you make it without that 5%? If God allowed you to divorce, would you be okay without that 5%?" Then she walked away. Proof had never really thought of it that way. Scar did many things and was still a work in progress, but could she give up his 5%?

The time came for Proof and Scar to finalize their divorce, but instead she and Scar went to lunch to celebrate their new beginning instead of going to the court. Proof figured that Scar and the first lady of the church were correct. Without Scar's 5%, she would not be all right. She and Scar did not finalize their divorce that day or ever.

Dear heavenly Father,

*Thank You for your love an• commitment to our marriage. Thank You, Lor•, that you are the thir•-string within the cor• in which my husban• an• I are intertwine•. Thank You, Go•, that just as **Ecclesiastes 4:12** states, we are not easily broken. Thank You, Go•, for saving my marriage an• not allowing the cankerworm an• locust to •estroy it. Thank You on the •ays that we feel like giving up that you will remin• us of the love that you have for us an• quickly realign our thoughts to your promises. Thank You, Go•, that You will*

teach us how to be servants of one another an• that we fin• pleasure in the way
that we serve each other because as we serve one another, we are serving you.
We are •isplaying to our mate your love for them through our service accor•-
ing to **Ephesians 5:33**. *Thank You, Go•, that we are equally yoke• abi•ing on*
your foun•ation.

It is so. In the name of Jesus, we pray. Amen

Awe! Scar and Proof finally have their happily ever after, or at least one would think. However, one of the saddest truths about Scar and Proof was their romance only lasted for a few short moments, then something always happened to bring turmoil to their happy union. Both desired the other, and neither liked to be apart but, neither understood how to remain in the fight. One would make a choice that never coincided with their marriage, and out of fear, Proof would bail on their commitment and Scar would become more numb. Unfortunately, their happy reconciliation soon turned into another devastating separation.

7

Proverbs 2:16

Chapter 7

"Wisdom will save you also from the adulterous woman, from the wayward woman with her seductive words." Proverbs 2:16

Proof woke up on her prayer room floor. Lately, she has been sleeping there nightly. Scar's absence had grown to two and a half years, and Proof's body yearned for him to the point of being extremely sore. She prayed and cried herself to sleep nightly. She had become very persistent in her prayers for God to answer, and she was not willing to let go of His hem until she received her breakthrough. Proof knew that her prayers were not in vain. She was standing on God's promises, and he had to honor His word and come through.

Scar would always become upset and then leave from time to time, but this was the first time he completely ignored her in his absence. In their past, Proof was always the one to stray for months to find clarity. She began to call him daily, which only resulted in no response. With each unanswered text or call, she began to feel useless and depressed. She attempted her hardest to hide her truth, but this time she had two children in high school, and the excuse of daddy being busy was growing just as old to them as it was for her to tell it. However, she would not confirm their accusations of their daddy leaving and living some-where else. She always turned it around on them to overthinking the situation.

She was glad it was Sunday. She could lay a few more moments in God's presence without having to rush to begin her day. By now, her children had learned she slept in the closet from time to time, and they thought she was crazy. She could care less. She was crazy! She was mad enough to believe that God would turn this crazy situation around, and she and Scar would live happily together in this beautiful home that God had provided.

By now, she knew her husband very well and was almost sure he had begun a new relationship with someone else. This was his pattern every time they separated. Proof would become engulfed with a fear that would push Scar away. Then Scar would begin something new somewhere else, only because he feared being alone. Proof could feel it by his nonchalant position every time they communicated. Proof could not help but think about another time this happened several years back, which resulted in Scar bringing a baby from another woman into their relationship.

December 2010

"Are you carrying me on your insurance?" Scar asked. Proof was slightly confused. What was this man talking about now?

"I have never carried you on my insurance, Scar. Why would I start now?" Proof asked. She was struggling to carry herself and their four children. He had his nerve! Not to mention this is the first time she had heard from him in weeks.

"I was just wondering Proof. I needed to know for something," Scar demanded. Proof knew that Scar was up to something. He could care less about some insurance. She could not help but wonder if he was sick or something.

"Why would you ask me that Scar, be honest," Proof continued. She was secretly hoping that if she continued to ask questions, he would tell her what was going on.

"None of your damn business Proof, as always, you worried about the wrong damn thing!" Scar scolded as he was hanging the phone up in Proof's face. Proof knew immediately from his demeanor the newest replacement had a tight grip on Scar's heart.

This replacement was unique. This woman was not the average. She was pulling Scar away mentally. Sadly, Proof would soon learn that this woman would be a carrier of Scar's seed.

Now what Go? she thought. Again, Proof had become very active in her church, and her prayer life began to elevate once more. She knew at this point only His move would change this damage.

People began telling Proof about Scar's infidelities and how he posted pictures of himself with this new replacement, and this conversation with Scar confirmed the rumors. Proof was receiving information so much that she began to grow weak and nauseous at the thoughts of Scar, sharing himself on an emotional level that he shared only with her. Proof asked all the flow of information to stop. Her soul could no longer take any more stories of Scar and the replacement. Proof was suffocating in a bundle of emotions and needed to come up for air.

She could hear the chime sound on her phone. It was a text message from Scar. It was not what the text said. It was what the signature block that brought her crashing down. In the signature block, it read *Ja*e's guy*. Why in the hell had he chosen to claim her home wrecking ass?

Proof did not respond to the text; however, she responded the best way she could. On her knees with prayer. She began to pray like she was fighting in a war. She could hear God saying, you know her name now call it out in prayer and reclaim your marriage.

Dear Heavenly Father,

*Thank You for Ja*e. Thank You, Father, because she is *rawing me closer to You, an* through my *rawing, it is also *rawing my husban* because we are of one flesh. Lor*, in Your wor*, you instruct that I *on't wrestle with flesh an* bloo* but with the Principality in high places (**Ephesians 6:12**). Thank You, Lor*, for having control over this battle. I alrea*y have the victory in your name. Thank you, Lor*, that the whore*oms spirit, accor*ing to*

*Proverbs 5:1-14, is boun♦, an♦ the pure heart, accor♦ing to **Ephesians 3:14**, is loose♦ in the name of Jesus. Thank you that the relationship between Scar an♦ Ja♦e is ♦estroye♦ in the name of Jesus. Thank you, Lor♦, that Ja♦e will fin♦ her own spouse to lay with an♦ not mine. For in your wor♦, it states that you will be the ju♦ge, **Hebrews 13:5**. Lor♦, thank You that you will ju♦ge them into conviction. Thank you, Lor♦, that what you have or♦aine♦ within my husban♦ an♦ me that no man can put asun♦er. Thank you, Lor♦, that you will also ju♦ge Scar into conviction for he has aban♦one♦ our marriage. Thank you, Lor♦, that Your will be ♦one within this relationship an♦ my marriage.*

It is so

In the name of Jesus, I pray.

Amen

Proof prayed this prayer daily. She transformed into a prayer warrior. She would wake up in the middle of the night just to pray for her relationship. She needed God to remove the taste of this woman from Scar. She needed God to restore her family. She needed God to return Scar to her. Proof began to recognize that she was indeed in a fight. Something deep inside her would not let her give up. She could hear God telling her, *♦on't give up on my son.* That alone was enough to make her remain in the fight.

"Momma" she heard a child calling. "I know we are not supposed to bother you, but we are hungry!" her youngest son shouted. Proof knew the time had come for her to leave her prayer oasis, plus she needed to hear the word today. She was all too familiar with unfaithfulness within the marriage. She needed a reminder from God that this battle was not one she was fighting alone. The thought of her husband sharing parts of himself that only belonged to her brought on a rage of unwelcomed feelings that only prayer could break.

All of the children were up and ready to move, waiting on food to complete their morning to her surprise. Proof decided that she would dress quickly and take the children out for breakfast. It was a beautiful day, and she needed a pick-me-up. She shook off the night ora and got her mind together to enjoy the encouragement that would be birthed from this day and her tiny morning dates. As always, she knew that her children would rekindle a fire that had escaped her throughout the night.

8

Genius 2: 24

Chapter 8

How healthy is your intimacy with your spouse? Do you appear to be one unit when seen by others?

"Therefore a man shall leave his father and his mother and hold fast to his wife, and they shall become one flesh" Genius 2: 24

"I want pancakes!"

"I want a T-bone steak!" Proof and Scar's children were not shy when it came to food. Proof would always joke about keeping a part-time job to afford the occasionally "happy meal" fund.

"Can I get hash browns instead of eggs?" Proof's children were hungrier than she imagined. They were acting as if the food was being delivered via a vending machine.

"Calm down and give the waitress a chance to collect herself," Proof begged her kids. Proof loved these types of mornings because it was the best way to talk with her children. She and Scar set the tone a while back for their children, allowing them to share whatever they liked with their parents understanding they were safe and loved.

As she looked at all three of her sons, she could see some resemblance of Scar in each one of them. Their oldest looked exactly like Scar; it was as if Scar was sitting in front of her. The middle was not the spitting image as his brother, but his mannerism was. He needed everything to be intact; he did not do confrontations well and continuously made sure his mother was always happy and not upset about anything. Scar hated when Proof was upset with him. He could ignore her, but he came unhinged when she did the same to him. The baby boy had all of Scar's personality and spunk. He was always moving, could never sit still, and very honest. If you were not searching for the truth, he was not the one to ask, for he was very truthful.

Proof continued enjoying her children this beautiful morning. "You all finish up so we can get to church," Proof instructed. As much as she was enjoying her babies, she did not want to miss the message for service today. She needed this message from God because she and Scar had been involved with the estranged women for too long. Proof gathered her children, paid the bill, and headed toward the church.

The service was phenomenal! Proof left the church with a proper understanding of God's heart toward marital life. Proof once thought that being intimate was the act of sex; however, she learned it is truly an act of oneness between a husband and wife, not easily broken after this message. It's a marital bond on display even when the marriage is taken away from the bedroom's quarters. It is the oneness established between spouses when they are alone as well as in the public eye.

The pastor gave the example of when he and his wife were apart while she was out of town visiting with family. He went on to say that in her absence, he missed her daily scents. Everyone chuckled because of where their mind wandered. He joked, "I got an audience of spiritual prevs."

He continued to share that he never realized how her daily scents gave him life. He said the smell of her shampoo was absent, the lotion and body spray she used once out of the shower were gone, the smell of morning coffee with a unique twist was not there, and the way the house smelled of freshly washed clothes when he returned from work was removed. He felt a sense of emptiness the entire time she was absent because the personal intimate smells he never realized were present suddenly were absent.

Once she returned, he shared how excited he was to spend the first night with her to wake to those familiar smells. Proof could relate. She had been puzzled about why she was so achy and pain-filled. However, after this message, she began to understand her body was in withdrawals. God designed marriage to resemble one unit. One should not be able to separate the units by looking at the two; it should always appear as one unit. It is almost like losing a significant piece of your body when a part of the unit is absent. Until that piece is repaired or returned, the other unit would remain in pain. Proof and Scar needed to be repaired. She needed her husband back because her pain was becoming unbearable and too familiar.

May 2011

"I cannot come back to you, Proof. She's pregnant with my baby," Scar said. Proof paused for a moment out of shock. This was the second baby that Scar and Proof did not share. The second time he had shared his seed with another estranged woman. The second time that Proof was going to have to watch another baby that Scar created grow up. Proof's heart began to shatter in her chest. She could feel everything in her body go completely numb. The feeling of defeat surrounded her like a choir with a horrible sound.

"Scar, I made a commitment to you with our marriage vows; this too shall pass," Proof assured. "Come home so that we can work this out," Proof promised. Scar did not say anything but goodbye.

March 2012

"Scar, I want you to come home so that we can talk about our future," Proof suggested. Scar had moved to another state. He had become exhausted with Proof and felt a new start would be beneficial.

"Proof I have no money, I lost my job," Scar announced. Scar was attempting to come up with any excuse. He needed Proof to lay off. He was under a strange commitment, and this time he could not remove himself at this point.

"That has never stopped anything before Scar, just come home," Proof said. She needed to see Scar; she had not laid eyes on him for some time now. Her life had become work, church, and prayer. That was the only way Scar would come back; however, she did not understand why God had not released him back to her yet. She was as faithful as she knew to be, but Scar was still fighting against her.

"Proof, are you gonna buy me a ticket or something?" Scar asked. He was hoping that Proof would not have the money. That would be his excuse not to come.

"Yes, of course, I am. I want to see you!" Proof exclaimed. That was all Proof needed was confirmation that Scar would come. She knew that once she saw Scar that a shift would instantly occur.

Proof was excited. She had a full night planned for Scar with fun and excitement. She made arrangements for their children, so there would be no interruptions. She also took off work, which Proof rarely did; she was ready to receive her husband. Scar's bus would be coming in at 4 pm, and Proof was already there waiting.

She could hear her phone ringing in the background. Once she picked it up, she could see it was Scar. "What's up, baby" she answered. "Are you almost here?" she said. All she wanted to hear was a strong yes.

"I missed the bus. I did not have anyone to take me to the station," he replied. Luckily Proof was always two steps ahead. She understood clearly by now how to read the excuse playbook written by Scar Moings.

"I figured this would happen. I bought you the type of ticket that you could change if needed. I can change your departure time to later today," Proof confirmed. She was not willing to have any excuses for this night being destroyed.

"Proof I can't come. I did not want to say anything, but I have something that I cannot change. Maybe next time," Scar quietly suggested. Proof sat there with that phone in her hands for hours. She cried until she had no more tears. She questioned everything about herself. Was she too fat? Was he no longer attracted to her? Was it over between the two? Would she ever have her husband back? Did this girl mean that much? At this point, she could no longer pray. All she could do was sob. She did not want to call anyone because everyone thought she was crazy. She usually used her children to mask the hurt, but they were already gone.

As she sat there being bathed in her tears, she could hear the Lord's voice say, "He is not ready, my daughter. His heart is still broken. He is attempting to repair his heart without you". All Proof could do was sob because she realized how much damage was caused at that very moment.

Proof started up her car, feeling empty. "However," God stated, "You can stand on my word and command victory in the name of Jesus". She backed the car up and pulled away, feeling defeated by her marriage. She later found out that Scar could not come because he welcomed his newest creation into the world. That news made her feel even more broken and defeated.

Proof remembered how God redirected her thoughts that day. She returned from that bus station fearless and with a God mandated courage. Every time she wanted to quit, she could hear the voice of God encouraging her.

Shortly after, Scar returned. He and Proof took their children on a vacation that allowed them to attempt to work through some differences. God had truly softened his heart, and he and Proof began to rely on one another. However, Proof stopped being a mandated prayer warrior for her marriage. Once Scar returned, her prayer closet rarely saw her, and going to church every Sunday became a chore. She stopped allowing herself to be fed by God.

There were times that Scar would suggest church, but Proof would make an excuse as to why they should not attend and spent the morning lying in Scar's arms. Their union appeared to be one; however, Proof forgot a significant part, God. She learned very quickly that not allowing God to have a position in their marital unit would again result in another heartache and, eventually, Scar's departure. She vowed to God right there that if He allowed Scar to come back again, she would not exclude Him ever again.

Dear Heavenly Father,

Thank You, Lor•, for forgiveness. For in the past, I have been unwise with my marriage. I no longer want to pluck my house •own with my han•s. I want to buil• it up with your wor•s, as state• in Proverbs 14:1. Thank You, Go•, that the barren spirit is remove• from my marriage, an• the spirit of unity is release•. Lor•, Your wor• tells me that whatever is boun• on earth is boun• in heaven, an• whatever is loose• on earth is loose• in heaven, accor•ing to Matthew 18:18. Lor•, thank you that the intimacy within my marriage is restore• fully. Go•, thank you that Scar will grab hol• of me as his wife, an• we will become one flesh uneasily broken or recognize• as a separate unit.

It is so. In the name of Jesus, I pray,

Amen

9

Colossians 4:6

Chapter 9

Does the way you communicate with your spouse build them up or tear them down?

"Let your speech always be gracious, seasoned with salt, so that you may know how you ought to answer each person" Colossians 4:6

Proof was ready to leave her entire family this morning. During the week, she received a reminder text from her church, informing her that Gary Chapman would be coming to speak about communication within marriage.

"You all need to come on!" Proof hollered. "I want to get a good seat. She grabbed her keys to make her way to the car, grabbing her *Prava* bag, Bible, and smallest child walking out the door.

Before she could get her daughter strapped in, she looked up to see five children running toward her truck. "You all almost got left. I do not want to be late," Proof laughed. "Everybody get your body strapped into the seatbelts. I am about to pull off!" Proof exclaimed.

Proof got into the church just in time. She was aggressive this morning for a good reason, the church was a full house, but Proof made in enough time to get a seat close to the front. Proof was well aware of Scar's love languages; it was for sure words of affirmation, physical touch, and quality time. She learned this long ago when she read the book, *The Five Love Languages*. She craved the wisdom needed to rebuild her faith to strengthen and save her marriage.

For many, the solution to her issue would be to abandon her marriage and Scar for good. However, Proof could not make such a drastic decision out of emotions without a clear prompt from God. She often desired to have a healthy friend base. One that would allow her to confess her desires and dreams of reconciliation openly. However, that was never her reality.

In the past, once her truth was revealed, her friend base gave ultimatums that required her to walk away without regrets. Therefore, she kept her marital affairs and worries to herself out of fear of others' unfiltered warnings.

The Holy Spirit instructed her to read the book *Proverbs* and concentrate on Scar's love languages. Proof became engulfed in this assignment. The fire grew daily within Proof because of her dedication toward seeing how God would turn this mess of marriage around.

After the choir finished with praise, her pastor got up to introduce Gary Chapman. Once up, Gary Chapman went on to talk about the importance of learning the language of your spouse. The text for his sermon was James 3:5-8. He strategically unpacked the meaning of James 3:8 *"But the tongue can no man tame; it is an unruly evil, full of ea•ly poison."* Gary Chapman spoke on the importance of being mindful of how you communicate with your spouse and how your communication can poison or speak life into your spouse forever.

"The tongue is the most powerful weapon within your marriage. One can use it for good and evil," Chapman instructed. "Sticks and stones will break my bones, but words... he paused, "they hurt," he continued. "Wives, I want you to understand that you hold more cards than you realize. As men we value your opinion and your praise," Chapman stated. "When we receive your praise we are like little boys on Christmas morning who just received our greatest wish. However, when we receive poisonous responses, we are like little boys that just lost our best four-legged companion," he advised. Proof immediately felt convicted in her spirit, thinking about past times she spoke venomous words over Scar. She immediately wanted to correct her wrong and make it right. Proof could not help but wish she would have heard this sermon years earlier in her marriage.

April 2014

"Scar, are you going to put together the shelves for me?" Proof asked. They were two months from having another baby, and Proof was ready to trade Scar in. One irritating truth about Scar, he was not to be rushed. He moved at his own pace.

"Proof, I told you I would when I get a chance. You cannot rush me," Scar said. Proof felt that Scar was doing this to get on her nerves. Scar knew that this baby was about to come soon, and Proof was growing anxious. Her anxiety level was through the roof, and Scar was about to raise it farther.

"Scar, you always do this to me. You got time to go out all night drinking and hang at your boys' houses during the day while I'm at work, but you don't have time to build some shelves. That makes no sense. I am sick of you! You are not going to amount to anything if you don't get your shit together! As soon as I have this baby, I promise I am leaving your ass," Proof angrily stated.

To make matters worse, Scar acted as if he did not even hear Proof talking, not to mention their children were standing there to witness everything said. He was sitting there looking at her as a clear glass window.

"You know what? I am about to go to my momma's house because I need a break. The kids and I are going to stay there for a while," Proof informed. Scar acted unfazed; he watched her pack up everything, big belly and all, while he sat there as his oldest son carried everything to the car. Scar looked relieved as the car pulled away from the sidewalk. Proof could not understand why Scar could care less.

May 2014

Proof had been at her mom's for about two weeks. During her time away, she came across the book *The Five Love Languages* by Gary Chapman. She took those two weeks to read it and learn that people have different ways of communicating. She realized that hollering at Scar would not give her the response she was looking for; it would only push him away. She decided it was time for her to come home. She and Scar had not talked much, but she felt it was time to return and continue to get ready for this baby.

When Proof walked through the door, Scar was not at home, but he had cleaned the house thoroughly and assembled her shelves. As she was picking up the phone to call Scar, he walked through the door. She was delighted to see him. The children ran past her to him. "Daddy," they screamed!

"Hey, Proof," Scar gently said. Proof realized at that moment that Scar was not her enemy, nor was he attempting to anger her. He was one that moved cautiously and not on demand.

"Hey, Scar," Proof responded. "The house looks excellent, and thank you for my shelves," Proof said. She was very impressed with Scar. He only needed a moment from her to think clearly, and that immediately saddened her.

"I told you I would get them done. You have to let me do me, Proof," Scar informed. What Scar never admitted to Proof was that he too was secretly reading Gary Chapman while she was away. He also secretly wanted better for his marriage. Proof was sorry for how she handled Scar before she left, but unfortunately, she never apologized nor admitted it to Scar; she just let it go. Even though Proof did not say sorry, she began to invest in various things that would improve the marriage, or so she thought.

After church, she and the children headed to dinner. Proof remembered how immature she had been in the past. She and Scar had no sound examples of what a healthy marriage resembled. She struggled with bridling her tongue when it came to Scar. He would always instruct her, "don't argue with me in front of my children," but Proof felt she had to get it out.

Proof made the difficult decision to contact Scar after lunch. She prayed that he would answer so that she could apologize for how she had handled her tongue in the past. She had to learn that the more she argued and put Scar down, the farther apart they grew. God had to teach Proof how to close her mouth.

Once home, she quickly settled her brew and ran off to her bedroom to make her long-overdue call. As the phone rang, she could feel her stomach dropping into the pits of her emptiness. Deep inside, she knew after the third ring that Scar was not going to answer. *Defeat again,* she thought. This reality was growing old, and Proof could no longer stand the harshness of Scar's disposition.

God gave her instructions to invest in intentional prayer for her marriage, and as she did, God whooped Proof into a conviction that led to repentance. She had to learn that it was okay to ask for forgiveness even if she felt the other party was wrong. She later learned that God would fight those marital battles if she would just let him.

Dear heavenly Father,

*Thank You for your mercies an♦ longsuffering. You offer forgiveness ♦aily. You sai♦ in your Wor♦ that we might have to ask to be forgiven seven times seventy times ♦aily. Thank You, Go♦, that You un♦erstan♦ I am not perfect an♦ offer me the grace of forgiveness. Teach me, Go♦, how to bri♦le my tongue an♦ not be the nagging wife You speak of in **Proverbs 21:9**. I want Scar in the be♦ with me, not on the roof. Thank You that the moment I begin to nag that I am convicte♦ back to your wor♦. Thank You, Go♦, that my wor♦s are seasone♦ with salt when I speak to Scar. Thank You that my communication with Scar speaks life over him ♦aily an♦ not poison. It is so!*

In Jesus name, I pray.

Amen

10

Ephesians 5:18

Chapter 10

Do either you or your spouse abuse drugs or alcohol?
"Don't be drunk with wine because that will ruin your life. Instead, be
filled with the Holy Spirit" Ephesians 5:18

September 2016

Scar and Proof were finally back together. It was Scar's favorite season of the year, football. Scar decided that he was going to take their boys to a game. Proof chose to go over to a family member's house to pass the time. The Classic is a football game that happens once a year between HBCU colleges. It is one of the most significant events that her city hosts.

Now that Scar has returned, Proof began noticing how quickly Scar was becoming a hefty drinker. The more he allowed himself to drink freely, the more unpleasant he became.

However, Proof figured that since the boys were with him, indeed, he would behave. Scar dropped Proof and their girl's off, as he left to begin his night of fun with his boys. The laughter and talk were soothing to Proof. She needed a mental escape.

The night began to grow old, and something in her soul was worried for some strange reason. Proof was pregnant with their sixth child, and she quickly blamed it on that.

Scar and Proof were attempting to relearn one another. Some days were more exhausting than others. She and Scar had recently moved into a new home. Proof felt blessed because they were granted section 8 housing, which was rare. This kind of grant was not usually given as fast as they received it. They were able to move their family into a three bedroom two bath home because of God's favor.

Before the move, Proof's prayer life, once again, became very consistent. She possessed the endurance to pray any length of time in all encouragement to save her family. Once they moved, however, Proof's prayer life began to weaken again. Those long talks with God started to get shorter, and her focus began to change. As Proof was listening to the current conversation with family, she realized the trust and motivation she once possessed for God was fading. Proof could feel a quiet tug at her heart from God telling her he missed her.

Proof and the rest of the family decided that everyone needed to lay down as the night was growing old. Proof decided to call Scar and check-in before she laid down. "Hello," Scar answered. There was so much noise in the background Proof could barely hear him,

"Hey, are you all on the way. I am ready to go," Proof hollered. Because Proof was so very pregnant, her back was beginning to hurt uncontrollably. All she wanted was a hot bath, her bed, and Scar's arms.

"Yes, baby, I am about to head out now," Scar replied. Right then, Proof heard in her spirit *tell him it's ok an♦ to stay; however,* Proof did not listen and said nothing. Proof felt that if Scar could make it to her, she would escort her family home. She shook off the strange feeling.

"Ok, come on, cause everyone is about to fall asleep over here." For some strange reason, Proof could not shake this feeling. Her stomach was in knots, and she could barely calm herself. Proof felt like something terrible was about to happen.

After about an hour of waiting, she knew something was wrong. Scar had not made it to her yet. She went to call but no answer. She called again, but no response. At this point, Proof was overly worried. She felt like crying. After about ten minutes of waiting, Proof could hear her uncle answering the phone, "Hello. What? I am on my way!"

Proof lay in the other room numb. A realm of nausea began surrounding her body like grief. Her uncle ran into the room with Proof and announced, "Proof, Scar and the boys have been in a horrible car accident." Proof jumped up, praying that her feelings were incorrect. She immediately ran to grab her shoes. Her uncle advised her that she could not go and to stay behind and wait on his return.

"I cannot go?" Proof shouted. Proof could not get herself to come to grips with everything that was happening. The room began to spin out of control, and the couch caught her fall, preventing her from hitting the floor. Proof was there physically, but her mind was at the accident site.

"This type of scene is not for a pregnant woman. I will go for you," her uncle stated. Proof sat back down, pretending to be okay with this choice. Proof was lost, she had no words, and she was beginning to have Braxton Hicks uncontrollably. The contractions were amazingly powerful! She could not pray. She could not run. She could not get her thoughts together. She could not even cry. She began to breathe, pace, and think to herself, *How are my boys? How is my husband? Is the car totaled?* She wanted to call out to anyone who would listen, but she couldn't. She just began to pray in the spirit. She was praying so fearlessly that she really could not keep up. She was full of the Holy Spirit. The enemy kept plaguing her mind. *Are your boys even alive? Did he kill them and him?* She stumbled to get a drink of water, praying that would calm her anxieties.

The phone rang startling Proof. "Proof?" her uncle says. *Is half of my family dead? How am I going to raise three children alone?* She thought.

"Yes," Proof weakly said. She sat there, tears streaming down her face bracing herself for the worst news. She looked around the empty room she sat for support; however, no physical help was present.

"The boys are fine; I got them. One has glass in his head, and one is slightly cut but, they are all fine," her uncle assured her. Proof immediately began to give God all the praise and honor. This night God had spared her family. She knew this was God's attempt to regain her attention. God is a long-suffering God, and He gives chance after chance. Proof understood, leaving God out of her union was a horrible omission.

"What about Scar?" Proof asked reluctantly. She prepared to brace herself once more. She felt that she and Scar had so much more to accomplish in this crazy union. She did not even want to consider the possibility of it being over.

"I honestly do not know. He is in the back of a squad car." Proof was filled with mixed emotions, glad that her husband was still alive but overwhelmed that her husband was going to jail.

Proof waited until her uncle got home with her boys, and all she wanted to do was hug them all night. She could not thank God enough for his grace and mercy. Once her boys fell asleep, her uncle began to inform her about this complex story. Scar was driving and hit a puddle of water; the car spun out of control and rolled over several times, sliding into a light pole. At this point, the police were not for sure if Scar was drunk, high, or both. Proof was furious! There is no way Scar was sober because he is a great driver. From that point on, Proof was deaf to the words being said to her. She began to grow more numb.

Proof sat there in a daze. As always, she drifted to a memory that caused unexplainable anxiety. The pastor was asking for couples to come up and pray for one another about addiction. Proof wanted to go so badly but did not want to stand alone. As she sat in her seat, she could hear the voice of the Lord saying *Scar, an· you are not in this alone. I am still here, an· I have never left you or Scar. I ha· to have that night occur because I misse· you, ·aughter, an· I nee·e· you to come back to me to save your family an· break the generational curses upon your bloo·line.*

Proof could feel her body tensing up. She went to stand and could feel her legs buckle under her. Just as she was about to fall, God sent an angel in human form. She touched Proof so sweetly and gave her the warmest hug she had not felt since Scar's departure. Proof buckled and laid in the unknown woman's arms and cried like her soul was on fire. At that moment, Proof did not care who saw, who questioned, or who approved. The woman was so warm and allowed Proof to just lay there in that moment. Proof could feel God removing all judgment and ridicule. Proof looked at the woman as she began to whisper in Proof's ear, "God knows, and He has heard your prayers. Be free from your pain and know that God will never leave you nor forsake you." And with that, the sweet angel walked away.

Proof wiped her eyes, thanking God for His grace and forgiveness. She quickly realized she had never forgiven Scar or herself for that night. Proof quickly mustered the strength needed to make her way to the altar to pray with the other couples. She knew deep down inside that something was breaking off of her marriage that had held her and Scar in bondage for far too long.

Dear heavenly Father,

Thank you for Your love and protection in my life daily. Thank you, God, that no weapon formed against my family, whether verbally or physically, shall prosper according to your word, **Isaiah 54:17**. *God, each day I leave my home I will wrap myself in Your whole armor each day, as stated in* **Ephesians 6:13**. *Thank You, God, that our family will soar so high in you that the principalities will come looking for us but find you. God, I command, declare, and decree that my family will not allow our life to be ruined by alcohol or any chemicals that alter our mind or body.*

It is so. In the name of Jesus, I pray. Amen

11

1 Corinthians 13:4-7

Chapter 11

Why did you say I do?

Love is patient; love is kind. It does not envy; it does not boast; it is not proud. It does not dishonor others; it is not self-seeking; it is not easily angered; it keeps no record of wrongs. Love does not delight in evil but rejoices with the truth. It always protects, always trusts, always hope, always perseveres.

1 Corinthians 13:4-7

Proof was sitting in church staring at the question; Why did you say I do? Many questions began to flow in Proof's mind. Why did she say I do? What made her want to marry Scar? What sparked her to fight to stay with Scar? She never thought about it before. Scar had not even proposed to her. Her union was created simply because she conceived out of wedlock, and their families insisted that marriage was the next step. She had to ask herself, Proof why did you say I do?

APRIL 2001

It was two weeks before Scar and Proof's wedding. Proof had recently given birth to their first child, and their family felt the next step was marriage; therefore, they decided to go through with it.

"Proof are you ready for marriage?" Scar asked. Proof was over the moon in love with Scar. She could not put it into words, but she knew Scar was the one. For some reason, she knew he would always take care of her. Shortly after the two graduated from high school, both decided to go their separate ways. Of course, Proof was devastated while Scar appeared unbothered. He went months without contacting Proof. When Proof finally made it to the point she could fall asleep without tears, she received a letter from Scar professing his love. That was all Proof needed to continue on her love quest with Scar.

"Yes, Scar!" Proof proclaimed. "Are you not ready to marry me?" Proof questioned.

"To be quite honest with you, Proof, I'm not. Marriage is a huge commitment that I do not think I am ready," Scar confessed. Proof immediately began to cry. Scar had been feeling uneasy about this decision the moment he agreed. Of course, he loved Proof, she was everything and more, but marriage was an enormous step.

"Why would you tell me this now? I thought this was what you wanted," Proof sobbed. Scar's confession felt like rejection. She could never imagine herself with anyone other than him.

"This is what I want one day, but not today and not right now," Scar announced. "We are too young, and we do not have a plan," Scar confirmed. Proof knew that Scar was right, but she was afraid that she would lose him. He was all Proof knew. He was everything to her. She could not explain it, but the way he cared for her was not something she was willing to abandon.

"Scar, you said that you would marry me and that you loved me. Why are you changing your mind?" Proof asked. Scar hated to hear Proof cry, and he hated even more to disappoint her. She was overwhelmed and not genuinely listening to Scar's concerns. All she heard was, "I don't want you anymore," which was beginning to break her.

"Proof, stop crying, and don't be upset," Scar said softly. "We can still get married," he announced. Proof's entire emotion changed from devastation to complete joy in a matter of seconds. She was excited to know that soon she would be able to call herself Proof Moings.

The night before the wedding, Proof, and Scar were supposed to be away from each other, but in authentic Proof and Scar fashion, they were not. "Proof, do you understand how serious marriage is to me?" Scar asked. Scar was willing to begin this journey, but he wanted Proof to understand how important this next step was. It was more than an arrangement.

"Yes, Scar, I understand," Proof responded. Proof understood that she and Scar were making a huge decision, but she had no clue about a wife's responsibilities.

Proof I cannot be more serious, marriage is one of the most important things I am going to do in my life, and I am not marrying to divorce," Scar announced. "We are about to become one whole. You have to understand that," Scar said. Proof had never heard Scar speak so seriously, everything was always a joke, but something in his voice screamed this is an unbreakable move. It made Proof a little alarmed. By the seriousness of his voice, Proof understood that marriage was no joking matter to Scar, but she struggled to understand why he was so forward. It was almost as if he was warning her. He was giving her the last opportunity to back out.

"Yes, Scar, I understand. It is just as important to me," Proof proclaimed. Proof and Scar did not have much. Therefore their wedding was held at a chapel in the mall. Not many attended because Proof and Scar had to pay for the attendees. However, everyone who mattered was present. Proof's mother and father, Scar's aunt and grandmother, and of course, their beautiful new baby girl were all in attendance. Proof was nervous; she could not be still. She kept walking all over the chapel going from one end to the other. "Ok, guys, let's get in position," she heard the officiant say. After about ten minutes, Proof became Mrs. Scar Moings, and she was elated!

As Proof sat there reminiscing, she glanced at the church altar to see all the newly engaged couples receiving prayer. How sweet, she thought. They all looked ready to embark on this thing called marriage. She yearned to run over to inform each couple that marriage is hard work, and the honeymoon only lasts a weekend, then the real work begins. She wanted to share with them that love can either be an emotion or a verb. Proof desired to tell them it's ok if you don't know how to respond to your spouse. As long as you both are willing to learn together. She wanted to yell, It's ok if you have to argue, but don't give up on the union that you are about to make no matter what. Put God first and keep your marriage between the two of you and never go to bed without communicating your differences and then praying about them.

Proof realized that she and Scar were not ready to get married. They were so immature and had no full understanding of what a healthy marriage required. That would explain why they struggled so hard with every peak and valley within their marriage. She quickly gathered herself, realizing that she had some unfinished business with her groom.

Proof was thinking on the way home from the church how she enjoyed and learned from the past series. She began this series thinking that she was going to learn why Scar was the way he was and how to change him, but instead, she learned how to respond to Scar. Proof learned that God uses each spouse as a vessel to represent Him. Every marriage is under a covenant guided by God. It's not fair to blame Scar without first examining herself or her actions. Proof decided that it was time to stop allowing Scar to be distant and visit him. She felt God nudging her to drop her pride and be the one to make the first move towards the repair of their marriage. Neither of them was correct to go this long without communicating, but one of them had to be the first to begin the restoration. She decided that she and the children were going to take a trip to visit Scar. Currently, Scar was working on an event that was three hours away from their home, so Proof chose to create a day trip for their visit.

Proof was given stringent instructions from God on how to handle her upcoming visit. God was not going to allow any evil spirit to prevent her from seeing Scar. God instructed Proof to apologize to Scar for her wrong in their marriage. God also told Proof to fast two days a week until 8:00 PM. She and Scar were married on the 27th. Therefore God ordered the second and seventh day of each week as mandated fasting days until their visit. Of course, everyone brought some form of yummy food to work, but her family restoration was far more critical than a donut.

Proof needed to inform Scar of their visit, so instead of calling him, she decided to text. She wanted to make sure that he was able to have a visual reminder that she was coming. Proof understood that a phone conversation could quickly switch around, but a text would be her personal documentation.

Hello, Scar. The chil•ren an• I will be in town in the next two weeken•s. I want to see you. Proof hit the send button, praying that the message would give Scar a clear visual of her plans. Scar did very well with turning her words around to meet his demands.

Scar immediately responded with; *I •on't think I'll be aroun•. I have to work.* That was always his excuse when he wanted to avoid Proof. She was irritated but understood that she was in God's will, and if God said so, it was so. *Are you working all night an• •ay?* She texted back.

Yes, Proof. That's all I •o, he responded.

"Scar, we will be in town for a day. Your children and I want to see you. I will text you when we arrive", Proof responded. Proof knew the more she went back and forth with Scar, the more irritated she would get; therefore, she ended the conversation.

It seemed as if those two weeks took forever, but the day finally had come for Proof to make her wrongs correct with Scar. She was excited to wake the children and get them prepared to see their father. It had been too long. Proof took considerable measures to make sure she looked pleasing to the eye.

As Proof stood in front of her floor-length mirror, looking at her reflection, she was pleased with the results. Her hair lay down her back, beautifully flat ironed, and she wore a form-fitted Maxi dress comfortable enough for traveling. Before walking away, she whispered, "Proof you have the victory." You are courageous. You are an excellent wife and mother. You will overcome this." She turned around, grabbed her

Richfresh gym bag for additional needs, and gathered her children for their day trip.

On the drive, Proof played gospel and love ballads. God was preparing her mind to receive the day. God orchestrated signs all while driving to confirm that she was in his will. God gave her butterflies, eagles that would soar in front or above her truck, and numbers. The entire way. She saw her anniversary date, 27, and the number 8, symbolizing new beginnings, repeatedly. At one point, she got behind a truck that had her wedding date 427 printed on the back. Proof was amazed at how God was moving. She could hardly wait to see what was in store for the day.

Proof and the children finally made it to the city. The children were growing antsy from the drive, and breakfast had worn off. She pulled over to grab a quick bite and contact Scar. To her surprise, he did not answer. Proof began to grow anxious, but God said, be patient, my daughter, and wait. She decided she would text in case he was working. Still no response. The children began to grow, even antsier and started whining and asking questions.

"I'm hot. I'm tired of sitting. Where is daddy?" Proof decided to take them to the park to ease her mind. She needed to allow them running time so she could sit and think. As she pulled into the park, she could feel a calmness come over her, as she heard God say, Do you think I brought you this far to leave you standing alone? Proof allowed the children to get out of the car to go and play.

She spotted a bench under a tree and decided she would listen to a sermon on YouTube while the children played. Before she could push play, her phone began to ring. She could feel her stomach almost leap out of her body. It was Scar. She sat there, holding the phone and just praising God for coming through for her. "Hello, sweetheart," Proof answered. She was praying

he was not going to give an excuse for this day.

"What's up? Where are you all at?" Scar said.

"We stopped at a park for the children to get out and run off some energy," Proof said. Plus, she needed a mental break from being cooped up in the car. Proof was enjoying the breeze, plus watching her children play brought joy to her heart.

"You should have stopped by and got me," Scar teased. It was evident in his voice that he was just as nervous as Proof. After all, it had been two years. He secretly wanted it to go just as perfectly as Proof.

"I will gladly come to where you are and pick you up," Proof promised. Proof was willing to complete any task needed to conquer her assignment given by God. Going to retrieve her husband was not a far-fetched idea.

"Send me your location. I am on my way," Scar stated. Proof's heart was beating through her Maxi dress. She was overly anxious to see her husband finally. At this point, Proof was like a young girl on her wedding day who had no idea of her future. However, she did not mind because she was in the will of God. He knew what he was doing.

One of her children ran over to her, "Momma, when are we leaving? I'm hungry again." At times it seemed that all her children did was eat. However, Proof proudly confirmed that their daddy was on his way and would be there soon.

When Proof looked up and saw Scar walking up, she had to prevent herself from bursting into tears because instead of seeing Scar walking, she saw the will of God operating. Before she could say one word, all of the children came running. They were happy to see him as well. Proof just sat back and allowed them to have their moment; she was thrilled that God had allowed this reunion to occur.

While Scar was embracing their children, he looked over at Proof in that way he always did. Proof could not do anything but smile. She could not hide her feelings, no matter how hard she tried.

Scar walked over to Proof and greeted her. "Hey, Proof." He then grabbed her, hugging with the warmth that she had desired for some time. Neither Proof nor Scar wanted to let go of this marriage. It began to seem as if their surroundings were spinning, and God was shifting the atmosphere.

Proof and Scar just remained there engulfed in one another with no words until one of the boys broke their concentration. "Are we about to go eat already?" he asked. Scar looked at Proof and asked, "Where do you want to go to eat?" Proof usually had more than enough suggestions, but today she could feel God saying allow Scar to lead. Wherever he goes, you follow without argument or complaint. Proof was never willing to argue with God; therefore, she agreed.

"Wherever you choose, Scar is fine with me," Proof said. Scar looked surprised that she was letting him choose. Proof always chose dining places. The family headed to lunch, and all of the children wanted to ride with Scar. Proof was okay with that because she needed a praise break that her children would never understand or comprehend.

Once at the restaurant, Proof was basking at the moment. To be able to watch the movement of God was priceless. Proof just sat back and watched Scar and their children. She was proud of herself for never tainting the image of their father. They were just as in love with him as she was.

"Daddy, I want a cheeseburger," One said. As always, Scar was willing to do whatever needed to please his family. That was never his issue. He struggled with comprehending how a woman that prayed like Proof, never trusting in her prayers. He grappled with how unchallenging it was for Proof always abruptly to leave when he made mistakes.

"Daddy, do you want to see the picture I drew on the way?" another said. One would never know that this family had been separated for two years.

"Daddy, can you get me some cleats for running?" their oldest son asked. She was taking it all in as if she were a bystander watching a beautiful family. Proof decided this was not the time to talk about the whys or how's. Now, it was time to enjoy the reunion of her family.

After lunch, Proof told their oldest daughter to walk their children to the ice cream shop in the same shopping center they were eating. At the same time, she and Scar went to get gas. She needed an excuse to be alone with Scar. Proof wanted to continue on her quest to complete the task God had given her.

It felt great to be alone with Scar. Her flesh wanted to ask so many questions, but God kept instructing her that it was not the time. God humbled Proof to the point of her feeling tears forming in her eyes, and she was trying her hardest to fight them away. She needed to say this without tears. She needed Scar to see her truth without her being emotional. She began slowly.

"Scar, I want to tell you I apologize for all the wrong I have done in this marriage," she said softly. A tear began to sneak down her face. His expression was priceless.

"What do you mean wrong?" Scar asked. Scar was confused. In his eyes, Proof did no wrong and especially not to him.

"I have made many mistakes, and I want to say sorry for them all," Proof continued. Proof wanted Scar to understand that he alone was not at the fault of their broken marriage. Scar was always willing to stay no matter how uncomfortable; however, Proof would leave prematurely. She struggled with staying and fighting through the rough.

"Did you do something that I don't know anything about?" he teased. Scar was attempting to lighten the moment. These types of atmospheres made him uncomfortable. Plus, he was secretly praying that Proof would not begin to question him.

"No, I know that my choice to continue to leave our marriage prematurely has pushed you away, and I need you to forgive me," Proof stated. Proof knew that she could not leave this moment without the grace of her husband's forgiveness. That would mean this entire trip would be in vain.

Scar absently said, "You are forgiven Proof." However, the look in Scar's eyes told Proof that he needed this moment. Proof felt a release like never before and calmness, knowing she had accomplished her God-given goal.

Once back with the kids, they allowed them to finish playing before Proof got back on the road. She needed them to be good and tired so that she could think about her day's results.

"Come on, children, let's go," Proof shouted. She would have stayed with Scar forever, but she needed to get back before too late. The family said a prayer together, and Scar hugged each child goodbye. Proof hugged and kissed Scar like it was the last time not releasing until she could no longer hold on.

On the drive back home, Proof thanked God for His presence and release on this day. She realized that she said "I do" out of force, but she stayed with Scar because of her commitment to God, and Scar. She made a vow to Scar to love him in sickness or health, and she made a vow to God to be His son's helpmeet. That meant that no matter what illness he had, she would be there. Through the beautiful times and the horrible, she would be there. She realized that it was not about her or Scar; it was about following God's will and how she represented God daily with her works. God revealed Scar's heart to Proof. The parts that loved his children unconditionally, the parts Scar gives to others without questions or restrictions, and most importantly, the part that hosted her. That alone was enough to encourage Proof to continue her fight. Proof did not know how God was going to work this thing called marriage out, but she knew she was in God's will, and no one was going to make her step outside of it, including Scar.

Dear heavenly Father,

Thank You for using me as your vessel. We are servants of You, and it is not our will God but Yours. You tell us to love our enemies because you make our enemies our footstools. I thank you, God, that a stool elevates one to reach something higher. God, I thank you for all the marriages around the world that struggle with trials and tribulations. Thank You, God, for giving them all the strength to endure this race; the race is not given to the swift but to the one who endures **(Ecclesiastes 9:11)**. *God, we are waiting upon you to renew our strength and give us wings to soar* **(Isaiah 40:31)**. *Thank You, God, for restoration in marriages.*

It is so. In the name of Jesus, I pray.

Amen